A *Perfect Landing*

Published in Nashville, Tennessee, by Tommy Nelson™, a division of Thomas Nelson, Inc.

Unless otherwise indicated, Scripture quotations are from the *International Children's Bible, New Century Version,* copyright © 1983, 1986, 1988 by Word Publishing.

Executive Editor: Laura Minchew; Managing Editor: Beverly Phillips. Book design by Kandi Shepherd.

Library of Congress Cataloging-in-Publication Data
Kirby, Lynn. 1956–
    Perfect landing / by Lynn Kirby
        p. cm.—(The winning edge series ; 1)
        Summary: Amy discovers that her relationship with Jesus is more important than competitive figure skating.
    ISBN 0-8499-5835-0
    [1. Ice skating—Fiction. 2. Christian life—Fiction.]
I. Title. II. Series: Kirby, Lynn, 1956–   Winning edge series ; 1.
PZ7.K633523Pe 1998
[Fic]—dc21

                                                                97–46714
                                                                CIP
                                                                AC

Printed in the United States of America
98 99 00 01 02 DHC 9 8 7 6 5 4 3 2 1

BOOK ONE
THE WINNING EDGE SERIES

A Perfect Landing

Lynn Kirby

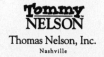

Tommy
NELSON

Thomas Nelson, Inc.
Nashville

For Sarah

Figure Skating Terms

Boards—The barrier around the ice surface is often referred to as "the boards."

Choreography—The arrangement of dance to music. In figure skating, it would be figure skating moves to music.

Crossovers—While going forward or backward, the skater crosses one foot over the other.

Edges—The skate blade has two sharp edges with a slight hollow in the middle. The edge on the outside of the foot is called the "outside edge." The edge on the inside of the foot is called the "inside edge."

Footwork—A series of turns, steps, and positions executed while moving across the ice.

Jumps

Axel—A jump that takes off from a forward outside edge. The skater makes one and a half turns in the air to land on a back outside edge of the opposite foot. A *Double Axel Jump* is the same as the axel, but the skater rotates two and a half times in the air. For a *Triple Axel,* the skater rotates three and one half times.

Ballet Jump—From a backward outside edge, the skater taps the ice behind with the toe pick, and springs into the air, turning forward. The jump appears as a simple, graceful leap, landing forward.

Bunny Hop—A beginner jump. The skater springs forward from one foot, touches down with the toe pick of the other foot, and lands on the original foot going forward.

Combination Jump—The skater performs two or more jumps without making a turn or step in between.

Flip Jump—From a back inside edge, the skater takes off by thrusting a toe pick into the ice behind her, vaults into the air where she makes a full turn, and lands on the back outside edge of the other foot. A *Double Flip Jump* is the same as the flip jump, but with two rotations. For a *Triple Flip,* the skater makes three rotations.

Loop Jump—The skater takes off from a back outside edge, makes a full turn in the air, and lands on the same back outside edge. A *Double Loop Jump* is the same as the loop jump, but the skater rotates two times. For a *Triple Loop Jump,* the skater completes three rotations.

Lutz Jump—Similar to the flip jump except the skater takes off from a back outside edge, thrusts a toe pick into the ice, makes a full turn in the air, and lands on the back outside edge of the other foot. Usually done in the corner. A *Double Lutz Jump* is the same as the lutz jump, but with two rotations. A *Triple Lutz Jump* is the same as the lutz jump, but the skater makes three full rotations.

Salchow Jump—The skater takes off from a back inside edge, makes a full turn in the air, and lands on the back outside edge of the other foot. A *Double Salchow* is the same as the salchow, but the skater makes two full rotations. For a *Triple Salchow*, the skater makes three rotations.

Toe Loop Jump—The skater takes off from a back outside edge assisted by a toe pick thrust, makes a full turn in the air, and lands on the back outside edge of the same foot. A *Double Toe Loop* is the same as the toe loop jump, but with two rotations. For a *Triple Toe Loop*, the skater makes three full rotations.

Waltz Jump—The skater takes off from a forward outside edge, makes a half turn, and lands on the back outside edge of the other foot.

Moves in the Field—Figure skaters must pass a series of tests in order to advance to each competitive level. These tests consist of stroking, edges, and turns skated in prescribed patterns. Sometimes referred to as Field Moves.

Spins
Camel Spin—A spin in an arabesque position.

Combination Spin—The skater changes from one position to another while continuing to spin.

Flying Camel—A flying spin. The skater jumps from a forward outside edge and lands in a camel position rotating on the backward outside edge of the opposite foot.

Layback Spin—A spin that is completed with the skater's head and shoulders leaning backward with the free leg bent behind in an "attitude" position.

One-foot Spin—An upright spin on one foot.

Sit Spin—A spin performed in a "sitting" position, on a bent knee with the free leg extended in front.

Two-foot Spin—The first spin a skater learns. The skater uses both feet.

Shoot-the-duck—One leg is extended in front while the skater glides on a deeply bent knee.

Skate Guards—Rubber protectors worn over skating blades when walking off ice. Also called blade guards.

Spiral—The skater glides down the ice on one foot with the free leg extended high in back.

Spread Eagle—The skater glides on two feet with toes pointed outward.

Stroking—Pushing with one foot, then the other, to glide across the ice.

Three-turn—A turn on one foot from forward to backward or backward to forward. Traces a "3" on the ice.

Toe Picks—The sharp teeth on the front of the figure skating blade. Used to assist in turns, jumps, and spins.

Zamboni—The large machine used to make the ice surface smooth.

One

As she circled the ice one last time, Amy Pederson glanced up at the clock. The skating session was almost over, but she wasn't ready to quit just yet. *If it kills me, I'm going to land this jump today,* she told herself.

Amy had been working on the double lutz* jump for months, and she had the bruises to prove it. Although she had often come close, she still had not succeeded in landing it. For the jump to be correct, a skater must complete two full rotations and land cleanly on one foot.

Amy stopped for a moment to think through everything she had learned about the double lutz. She reached up and tucked in the wisps of pale blond hair that had escaped from her ponytail. Her tights were soaking wet from the many falls she had taken on the ice that afternoon, and her cheeks were pink from working so hard.

---

*An asterisk in the text indicates a figure skating term that is in the list of definitions on pages v-viii.

Amy was tired. As always, she woke up by 5:15 and was at the ice rink for skating lessons by 6:00 A.M. After her lessons, she showered and dressed for school, and by 8:00 A.M. she was in homeroom. After school she returned to the rink to practice until the last freestyle ended at 6:00 P.M. She glanced at the big clock across the rink. *Fifteen more minutes until this session is over,* she thought. Nevertheless, she was determined to land a double lutz before she went home.

This is it! she thought, as she took a deep breath and jumped back onto the rink. Watching for other skaters, she skated backward straight into the corner of the rink. With her left arm forward and her right arm back, she extended her right leg straight behind her, thrust her toe pick* in the ice, and vaulted high in the air. Once, twice, she spun around before coming down smoothly on her right blade.

"Yes!" Amy shouted excitedly. Several other skaters looked at her curiously, but she didn't care. She had landed the jump perfectly! . . . And just in time.

"Skaters, the freestyle has now ended," came the announcement over the sound system. "Please clear the ice."

A few kids continued skating, ignoring the announcement; but now that Amy had landed her jump, she was ready to go. She slipped her skate guards* over her blades and headed for the locker room.

"Hurry up, Amy!" Her friend Elizabeth already had her skates off and was ready to go. "Mom's picking us

2

up early tonight, remember?" Elizabeth Martinez was a pretty Hispanic girl with an olive complexion and dark hair and eyes. The two girls had been best friends for as long as Amy could remember. They had even started skating together when they were both seven years old. Since they lived in the same neighborhood, their mothers took turns driving them to skating practices. This afternoon Mrs. Martinez was driving.

"I'm sorry, Elizabeth, I forgot!" Amy sat down on a bench and hurried to take off her skates. She looked up and grinned, her hazel eyes sparkling. "Guess what? I landed my double lutz!" she bragged.

Elizabeth pretended to pout. "That's not fair! I've been working on that jump for months, and I still can't get it."

"I'll be glad to help you," Amy teased. "After all, I'm an expert now!"

"Yeah, right! Land one jump and she's an expert!" Elizabeth rolled her eyes.

Amy grinned at Elizabeth. All kidding aside, she knew she could always count on her friend's support. Even when they competed against each other, they refused to allow it to interfere with their friendship.

It has been a perfect day, and nothing is going to spoil it, Amy thought. On the drive home, Elizabeth chattered about something that had happened at school; but Amy hardly heard her. She was too excited about landing the double lutz to think of anything else.

For the last few years, skating had been Amy's life. Now that she was in middle school, it was getting harder to say no to all the activities in which her friends were involved. But Amy didn't mind. She truly loved the sport, and her instructors seemed to think she showed real talent. And now that she had landed the double lutz, her next jump would be the difficult double axel*. Amy was feeling really good about her skating. All her hard work was beginning to pay off. *Wait 'til Mom hears,* she thought.

But the moment Mrs. Martinez pulled into the Pederson driveway, Amy sensed something was wrong. Her mother, who worked part-time in the mornings, was always there when Amy or her brothers came home from school and sports practices. Yet today the house looked deserted. Amy remembered the spare key her mother had pinned inside her school bag for emergencies. She had never needed it before. Nervously, she took it out of the bag.

Mrs. Martinez looked worried. "Why don't you come on over to our house until your parents get back? I don't like leaving you here alone."

"No, thanks," said Amy with more assurance than she felt. She climbed out of the car with her skate bag over one shoulder and reached for her backpack. "I'm sure they'll be back soon. Mom probably had some errands to run. See you tomorrow, Elizabeth. Thanks for the ride."

Amy gave her friends a reassuring smile. Mrs. Martinez waited until Amy had let herself into the house. Once in the door, Amy waved good-bye and Mrs. Martinez drove off.

"Mom? Joe? Kurt?" she yelled. No one answered. It seemed strange that even her brothers were not there. Joe should be getting ready for hockey practice, and Kurt's elementary school was out long ago. The stillness of the house was scary. Amy had never really been home alone before.

She couldn't find any notes explaining the mysterious whereabouts of her family. *They probably just forgot to tell me about one of the boys' meets. They'll be home soon,* she thought.

Amy toted her things upstairs and changed into jeans and a big sweatshirt. Then she went down to the kitchen to find something to eat. It seemed ages since she had eaten lunch, and she was hungry.

Amy found some ham in the refrigerator and made herself a sandwich. But before she could take a bite, the phone rang. Amy jumped to answer it—maybe it would be her parents.

It was her mother, and from her voice Amy immediately knew something was wrong.

"Amy, your father's been in a very bad accident." She paused, and Amy thought her heart would stop before her mother could finish. "A car hit his car while he was driving home from work this afternoon. He's in surgery now. The boys and I are at the hospital."

There was a long pause. "Is he okay?" Amy finally blurted out.

Amy realized that her mother was close to tears.

"He's alive, Amy. That's all we know. We're still waiting to talk to the doctor—"

"Mom, I want to come to the hospital!" Amy yelled.

"I'm sorry, but I can't leave right now. Amy, I tried to reach Elizabeth's mother but no one was home. I talked with Mrs. Lang next door, and she said you are welcome to spend the evening with them. Would you like to do that?"

"No."

"I hate to leave you home alone," her mother said, then sighed. "Well, if you need anything you call Mrs. Lang. I'll call you back as soon as I hear something. . . . Amy?"

"Promise?" asked Amy.

"I promise I'll let you know something as soon as I can. Don't leave the house, and be sure all the doors are locked."

Amy hung up the phone and sat down to eat her sandwich, but suddenly she wasn't hungry anymore. She couldn't imagine her strong, energetic father lying helpless in a hospital bed. Once when she was a small child her father had broken his leg skiing. Even now she remembered his jokes about the cast he wore. *Would he be joking about this soon?* she wondered.

Amy went into the living room and turned on the television, hoping to take her mind off her worries. It didn't do any good. She stared blankly at the screen, hardly knowing what was on. Finally, she fell asleep on the sofa.

Amy woke with a start when she heard the key turn in the front door. She was relieved to see her mother and brothers come in, but her relief soon turned to new fear. She could see by the troubled expression on her mother's face that things were not okay. Joe looked suddenly grown-up, and Kurt's eyes were red.

Amy's mother sat down on the sofa and wrapped her arms around Amy as she told her that her dad was in a coma, and the doctors were not sure if he would survive. For the next few days, the family hovered in the hospital waiting room. School, skating, and hockey practices were pushed aside.

It was a week before Mr. Pederson awoke from the coma, but he was still close to death.

Two weeks after the accident the family was finally given some good news. Amy's father was going to live. However, his spine had been seriously injured. At the very least, he would be in a wheelchair for several months. It was more likely that he would never walk again.

Amy couldn't believe what was happening. At first she was relieved just to have her father out of danger. But as the weeks passed she found herself wondering about the new family routine and when things would return to normal.

By the time Mr. Pederson came home from the hospital, Amy and her brothers were beginning to catch up on their schoolwork. The boys resumed their hockey practices, and Amy started skating again. Things seemed to be getting back to normal. Amy was sure her dad would prove the doctors wrong. He would be walking again soon—she just knew it.

However, months passed and there were few signs of improvement. As a self-employed businessman, her dad's job required him to travel. His back injury made that impossible. Slowly, he began laying off employees, and finally he was forced to close his business. He was left without a job, and his health insurance was running out.

* * * * *

One afternoon Amy came home from skating practice to find her parents sitting in the kitchen in front of a stack of letters and bills. Although she had heard some heated words before she came in, her mother and father became silent when they saw Amy. Too silent.

"What's up?" Amy asked, puzzled. No one answered.

Amy shifted uncomfortably, looking from one parent to the other. She suddenly realized how much older they seemed than before her dad's accident.

Mrs. Pederson's shoulder-length blond hair was pulled neatly back. Amy had always been proud of her mother's classic looks and good taste. But now there were dark circles under her eyes and lines on her face that Amy was sure had not been there before.

However, it was her father who had changed the most. Always full of life, he now seemed pale and shrunken in his wheelchair. His gray eyes had lost their twinkle, and his dark blond hair showed touches of silver. The long months of illness had taken a heavy toll. Amy wondered, *Will he ever be himself again?*

Finally, her mother spoke. "Amy, I'm afraid we've got some bad news," she began.

"Linda, let's hold off on this," pleaded her dad.

"No, we might as well get it over with." Mrs. Pederson looked at Amy. "Honey, we're going to have to make some changes."

"Changes?" asked Amy.

Her mother took a deep breath. "We have a lot of bills, and your father is not going to be able to work for a long time. I'm going to look for a full-time job, and we still have some savings, but that's not going to be enough."

"I'll help as much as I can," Amy offered. "And I'll try not to ask for anything I don't really need."

Her mother tried to smile. "Thank you, Amy. I know we can count on you. But I'm afraid there's more." She glanced toward her husband, who was looking down.

"What else?" Amy had a sudden sick feeling. Skating was an expensive sport. Would she have to cut back on her lessons and practice?

Mrs. Pederson cleared her throat. "We're moving to Texas to be near your grandparents in Walton. We're going to need their help to take care of your father during the day and take him to therapy."

"There's not a skating rink in Walton!" Amy panicked. This was worse than she thought. But her comment was met only by silence.

"Joe and Kurt will have to give up their hockey," her mother reminded her. "And Joe just made the freshman basketball team. We're all having to make some sacrifices."

"But that's different! Joe can play basketball in Walton!"

"I'm sorry, honey. Maybe later on you can go to Dallas to skate," her mother said softly. "But in any case, you will need to stop skating for a while. You know skating is expensive. We just can't afford it right now."

"Stop? I can't just stop!" protested Amy. "You don't understand. It will ruin all my chances of becoming a top skater if I stop now!" Amy was too upset to notice the look of pain on her parents' faces.

"I'm sorry, Amy," said her father quietly. "We'll try to have you back on the ice as soon as we can. We promise."

"Yeah, when I'm thirty!" Amy was trying hard not to cry, but she wasn't succeeding. "Never mind, I was going to quit skating anyway!" she shouted as she ran upstairs to her room. She slammed the door and burst into tears. *They just don't understand,* she thought. Amy felt like her life was over.

Two

Amy sat down in her new bedroom and pulled out the stationery Elizabeth had given her. Writing to Elizabeth helped to keep away the loneliness she felt.

January 25

Dear Elizabeth,

> *I don't know how I'm ever going to stand living in Walton. The nearest skating rink is thirty-five miles away. It might as well be on the other side of the world! I haven't been able to skate even once in the three months we've been here. Mom is busy with her new job, and of course Dad can't go anywhere.*
> *Joe and Kurt don't seem to miss Glenview at all, even if they can't play hockey here. Joe made the high school basketball team, so he thinks he's really cool. And Kurt is playing in a community soccer league.*

The only nice thing about living in Walton is being close to my grandparents. I've never been able to spend time with them before. Grandpa takes Dad to therapy every morning so Mom doesn't have to take time off her job. And Gram sometimes comes over in the afternoon to fix dinner for us.

Walton Middle School is okay, but the kids aren't very friendly. Nobody knows anything about skating. When I tell people I'm a skater, they look at me like I'm from another planet. I sure miss you and all the other kids at the rink.

Love,
Amy

Amy finished her letter and found a stamp.

Without skating, she felt so lost. Moving to a new school where there were no skaters made it worse. Somehow she just didn't fit in. The other girls, only interests were boys, music, and clothes. *Surely they must realize there is more to life,* thought Amy. *Like skating.*

She put the letter on her dresser to mail the next day and looked around her room. Reminders of her skating days were everywhere. Medals from various competitions and ribbons of different colors were displayed in a special case her father had made for her. Her skate bag stood in the corner—although she hadn't been skating in months, she refused to hide it away.

The walls were covered with posters of Amy's favorite skaters. Some of them were pencil sketches she had done herself. Now that she wasn't skating, Amy had more free time than ever before. The last few months she had spent many hours drawing pictures of what she couldn't do anymore.

Amy pulled out one of her skating magazines and flipped through it, looking for a picture to sketch. Finally, she settled on a picture of a skater doing a lay-back spin*. She picked up a pencil and her sketchbook and went to work trying to copy freehand the beautiful position of the girl in the picture—imagining she was the girl.

By the time her mother tapped on her door, the picture was almost completed. "It's time for supper," Mrs. Pederson called through the door. Reluctantly, Amy put down her drawing and went into the dining room.

The aroma of garlic, tomato, and cheese came from two large boxes on the dining room table. Amy's brothers were already there, waiting impatiently. "Mmm, pizza!" said Amy, as she sat down. "What did we do to deserve this?" She looked at her parents, who sat silently grinning.

"They won't tell," complained Kurt. "Not 'til you got here."

"Okay, out with it," demanded Joe. "Amy's here now."

Mr. Pederson spoke. "All right, I guess it's time for some good news for a change." He looked at his wife and smiled. "First of all, the doctors told me today that they think I've made some significant progress. With some more therapy, I should be ready to begin using a walker soon."

"Way to go, Dad!" cheered Joe.

"All right!" Kurt chimed in.

Amy waited expectantly. From the look on her dad's face, she could see there was more.

Mr. Pederson continued. "Next week I'm starting a new job." He paused a moment to let the news sink in. "It doesn't pay very much, but it could lead to something better in the future. Besides, it sure beats staying at home and watching television."

"Will you have to go to an office?" asked Amy.

"Yes. Your grandfather will take me there after I'm finished with my morning therapy, and your mother will pick me up on her way home from work." He looked at the pizza. "Well, what is everyone waiting for? Let's dig in!"

Amy munched on her pizza without saying much. Her mother and father looked happier than she had seen them in months. It made her feel guilty that she couldn't share their joy. She knew she should just be glad that her father was better, and she was glad. But Amy couldn't help wanting more—she wanted to skate again. Even if there were enough money for skating, the nearest rink was almost an hour away. How could she possibly get there? It just seemed hopeless.

❋ ❋ ❋ ❋ ❋

Gram usually shopped in the grocery store nearest her home, but this afternoon she was driving in the opposite direction.

"Why are we going this way?" Amy asked her grandmother.

"The Big Apple is having a triple coupon special," her grandmother said.

To get to the Big Apple grocery they had to cross the main highway that ran through Walton. As they approached the interstate, Amy spotted a sign in front of a large empty lot. She gasped. The sign read: "Future site of The North Texas Ice Palace—opening in June." She read it again to herself, then yelled, "Gram, stop!"

"What?" asked her grandmother, as she put on her brakes and jerked to a halt.

"They're building a rink!"

"Amy, don't scare me like that! I nearly ran through the intersection," scolded her grandmother.

"But, Gram," explained Amy, "they're building a rink!"

"What are you talking about?"

Amy pointed toward the empty lot and the sign. "Over there. The sign says they're building a skating rink—and it's going to open in June. Gram, I can skate again!" Amy's face lit up with a broad smile.

"It's probably another roller rink," replied her grandmother, as she took off toward the intersection.

"No," Amy insisted, shaking her head firmly. "It said, 'Ice Palace.'"

Her grandmother looked doubtful. "That's the first I've heard of it." She glanced at Amy and smiled. "But I hope it's true."

Amy didn't say anything else. She was too busy making plans. She wasn't sure if her family could afford for her to begin skating again, but she knew she could find a way if she only had ice.

❄ ❄ ❄ ❄ ❄

The prospect of a new skating rink gave Amy hope. Every chance she got, she persuaded her mother or grand-parents to drive past the construction site. However, it was months before much happened. By late winter, the site was still mostly dirt, and she began to wonder if the rink would ever be finished.

By the time the sign finally went up announcing its grand opening, it was nearly September. Almost a year had gone by since Amy had last been on the ice.

Shortly before opening day, Amy got out her old skates. She looked them over. She knew there was no way to get new ones. Amy held her breath as she tried them on. She breathed a sigh of relief as she squeezed each foot into its skate. Fortunately, her feet didn't seem to have grown too much. It was a good thing. Rental skates were fine for beginners, but she couldn't imagine trying to perform advanced figure skating moves in rental skates. Eventually, of course, she would have to have new skates, but she wouldn't worry about that now.

Amy couldn't wait to get back on the ice again. Still, as she waited for the new rink to open, she couldn't help wondering: *Will I still be able to do my jumps?*

Three

On the day that the new rink opened, Grandmother Pederson dropped Amy off at the rink door. She asked uncertainly, "Do you want me to stay?"

Amy reached for her skate bag. "No, thanks, Gram. Mom promised to pick me up on her way home." She waved to her grandmother, then headed inside.

A blast of cold air greeted her when she pulled open the door. It felt wonderful after the heat wave of the last few days. Amy paid her admission and wandered into the foyer. She hoped that she didn't look too conspicuous. At her old rink in Virginia she would have worn a skating dress, but on the first day she wanted to blend in with the crowd. She had decided on leggings and a big sweatshirt.

After lacing her skates, Amy looked around at the newly built rink. The long entrance foyer had a number of low benches, and a skate counter stocked with rental skates lined one side. At the far end was a snack bar with a few tables. The ice surface was visible through a long wall of windows, and Amy could see several people already on the ice.

It was obvious that most of the kids there had never been on ice skates before. Amy watched as a group of boys from her school wobbled toward the ice. Their skates were tied so loosely that they could barely walk—even on the floor. Amy wondered how they expected to skate that way.

One by one they stepped onto the ice, clinging to the boards and each other. They didn't stay upright long, however. The biggest boy in the group, known as the school bully, suddenly tumbled to the ice, grabbing the nearest boy. Amy giggled as the boys dropped like dominoes, one after another.

Just wait until they see what I can do, she thought to herself. Even though she hadn't skated in months, she was sure she'd outskate these kids. So she was a little disappointed when she noticed a couple of kids working on jumps and spins. Amy watched as a tall, auburn-haired girl executed a double flip jump*. She wondered how there happened to be figure skaters in a town that had never before had an ice rink.

Amy pulled on a pair of gloves and headed for the ice. But before she could get on, a jeering voice sounded across the arena, "Wimpy jump!"

Startled, Amy looked up to see a freckle-faced boy with red hair standing at the side of the rink. He skated over to the auburn-haired girl, and Amy realized that they looked almost exactly alike. Amy figured they must be brother and sister.

"You call that a double flip?" scoffed the boy. "I can do better than that!"

The girl seemed more amused than annoyed. "Okay," she said with a grin. "Let's see you try."

"All right." The boy stroked confidently around the rink, taking longer than necessary to set up for a double flip jump*. When he finally went for the jump, it was high and strong. Unfortunately, he missed the landing and slid along on his rear end until he hit the wall.

"Ouch," he said, as he picked himself up off the ice.

"Lovely jump," teased the girl. "But, silly me, I would have landed on my skate blade. You land your way, I'll land mine!"

"At least I *jumped!*" he retorted, determined to have the last word. "Your jump barely got off the ground!"

Rather than getting angry, the girl simply turned and began settingup for another double flip. This time she put extra energy into her takeoff. The jump was high, clean—and perfectly landed.

Amy had to smile at the boy's expression. She could see that he was annoyed, but rather than admit defeat he merely started working on something else. Amy felt sure that he would soon challenge the girl on some other move.

It's time to quit watching those two and get to work. Amy took a deep breath and wondered whether her jumps would be wimpy or merely nonexistent. She paused at the barrier long enough to take off her blade guards; then she glided onto the ice and began stroking slowly around the rink. At first she felt a little shaky, but soon she was building up speed. It felt good to skate again.

For the next hour, Amy reviewed every move she could remember—starting with the easiest turns and spins. Little by little she gained confidence as she was able to complete moves she had worked on for years. Of course, everything needed a lot of work, but for the first day she was pleased that she could skate at all.

The jumps were more discouraging. Amy had mastered most of the double jumps before she quit skating, but now she found it difficult to perform even the single jumps, which require only one full rotation. Most disappointing of all was the axel*, a difficult jump in which the skater takes off going forward and makes one and a half turns in the air before landing backward. Amy had worked many months to learn that jump, and now she could not do it at all.

Finally, Amy took a break. Only then did she realize how tired she was. It was time to call it quits for the day. Finding a bench, she sat down to unlace her skates.

"Hi!" said a friendly voice. Looking up, Amy saw a warm smile and sparkling brown eyes. It was the auburn-haired skater she had watched earlier. "I haven't seen you before," the girl said. "I thought Kevin and I were the only skaters in Walton."

"Kevin?"

The girl pointed out the red-haired boy who had teased her about her jumps. "Kevin is my twin brother. Not that I'm always thrilled to claim him."

Amy grinned. "Do you live here in Walton?"

"Yes, but we've always skated at the rink in Richardson. Until now, of course."

Amy's eyes grew wide. "Richardson! That's thirty-five miles away!"

The new girl smiled. "That's why I'm so excited about our new rink! How do you like it?"

"I love it," Amy said. Then she laughed. "Of course, I'd be happy with any kind of ice. I've been waiting for the rink to open for months and months. It's been almost a year since I've been on the ice."

"Where did you skate before?" the girl asked.

"In Virginia, but we moved here last fall."

"Well, I'm glad to find someone here who skates. I'm Kristen Grant. What's your name?"

"Amy Pederson."

"Will you be skating every day?" Kristen asked.

Amy didn't answer right away. She hated to admit it, even to herself, but money was still tight at home. She wasn't sure how often she would be able to skate since it cost money each time. "I don't know," she answered. "I wish I could, but . . ." She trailed off, unsure of how to explain. After all, she didn't really know Kristen.

But Kristen seemed to understand, or at least she had enough tact to change the subject. "Well, it will be great to see you sometimes, anyway," she said. "Do you go to Walton Middle School?"

"Yes. How about you?"

"I'll be starting there this year. The last three years my brother and I were homeschooled. I think I'll like going to Walton, though. What grade will you be in?"

"Seventh," said Amy.

"Me, too," said Kristen. "Maybe we'll have some classes together. Well, I'd better get back to work. Don't forget to look for me."

Kristen was a wonderful skater, and Amy watched her for a few minutes. She couldn't help being a little envious, but she was glad she had found a friend. She hadn't realized how much she missed having a skating friend.

When Mrs. Pederson came to pick her up a few minutes later, Amy was very quiet. "I thought you'd be excited to be back on the ice," her mother said.

"I am," said Amy, "but I'm so *awful!* I feel almost like a beginner."

"You knew it would take time to get back in shape."

"I know, but that doesn't make me feel any better. I'm going to need a lot of work if I'm going to get back to my old level." Amy sighed.

"Were there many people on the ice?"

"A few. One of them is really good. Her name's Kristen Grant. Her brother skates, too. They've been skating in Richardson."

Mrs. Pederson looked surprised. "That's a long way from here."

Amy shrugged. "I know. Kristen seems pretty serious about skating." She looked anxiously at her mother.

"Mom, I know we still don't have much money, but to get into shape, I need to skate every day."

Mrs. Pederson sighed. "I'm not sure we can manage that much skating, Amy. I'm sorry. Maybe by next year you can skate more, but for right now you will just have to manage with two public sessions a week."

Amy groaned. "Twice a week," she grumbled. "I might as well not bother."

Mrs. Pederson gave her a stern look. "If that's how you feel about it, perhaps you *should* forget it."

"I'm sorry, Mom, but I've lost so much time already. If I can't get back to a real practice schedule soon, I might as well forget about being a champion skater. And public sessions! You know that serious figure skaters don't skate in public sessions. There's no room to jump. There are kids every—"

"If you really care about skating, you'll take advantage of whatever time on the ice you can get," said Mrs. Pederson firmly.

Amy knew the subject was closed, but she also knew she had to skate more than twice a week. Being back on the ice again had only made her realize how much she missed it. As they pulled into the driveway, Amy decided there just had to be a way to skate more. If there was, she would find it!

Four

That night at supper, Amy didn't really feel like giving a report on her skating. She was glad the topic of conversation was school, which was starting the next week. Joe and Kurt were excited to be going back. Joe was fifteen and would be starting his sophomore year. Except when he hung around his high school friends, Joe was usually a pretty cool brother. Kurt was nine, going into the fourth grade. He was a bit pesky at times, but he wasn't too bad. On the whole, Amy got along well with her brothers, even though they did tease her.

While Joe and Kurt talked about seeing their friends and getting involved in sports practices, Amy listened a little enviously. She wished that she could share in their enthusiasm, but she couldn't help dreading the new school year. Walton, Texas, certainly wasn't anything like Glenview, Virginia.

"There's a new football coach at the high school," announced Joe. "Maybe we'll have a winning team for once." Walton's team was known for its record losses.

"Really?" said Mr. Pederson as he helped himself to the salad. "Who is he?"

"I think the name's Thompson. I heard that his last team won a regional championship."

"I met his wife," volunteered Mrs. Pederson. "She told me they just bought a house down the street."

"Cool," said Kurt.

Joe groaned. "I don't want any of the teachers living on our street. Especially a coach."

Mr. Pederson ignored Joe's comments. "Where did you meet her?" he asked.

"She's going to be working at our office," said Mrs. Pederson. "She seems very nice. They have five-year-old twin boys." She paused. "By the way, Amy, Mrs. Thompson mentioned she is interested in finding a baby-sitter for Friday nights."

"Friday nights!" protested Amy.

"Mrs. Thompson wants to go to the Friday night football games with her husband. She'll need a sitter, and I told her you might be interested."

"You said I wasn't old enough," said Amy.

"That was last year. You'll be thirteen in a month, and I would be close by if you needed help. I think it would be okay."

Amy frowned. "But Friday nights. I might like to go to the games!"

"You don't have to do it if you don't want to," said her mother, "but you've never been interested in going to the games before."

Amy reached for another roll. "I'll think about it."

All during dinner Amy thought about what her mother had said. The truth was that Amy didn't really feel comfortable around small children. However, the more she thought about it, she realized that this might be a good way to earn some money for skating. If she could get a lot of baby-sitting jobs, she might even be able to earn enough for some lessons. Maybe this was an answer to her problem. Amy began to get excited.

After supper, Amy offered to help her mother with the dishes. "Mom," she said, "I think I might want to try that baby-sitting job. I can use the money for skating."

Mrs. Pederson smiled. "That's why I told Mrs. Thompson you'd love to do it," she said.

"Mom! You didn't!" exclaimed Amy. Then she laughed. "I'll bet you asked Mrs. Thompson to give me the job."

Mrs. Pederson didn't say anything. She just grinned as she handed Amy a plate.

❅ ❅ ❅ ❅ ❅

On the morning school started, Amy awoke to the sound of dripping rain. *Great,* she thought, *I'll have frizzy hair for the first day of school.* She crawled out of bed and stared mournfully into the mirror at the pale blond curls hanging down her back. *Too bad we can't wear hats to school.*

Before her father's accident, Amy had followed the latest fads. But there was no money for trendy clothes these days. She put on a pair of jeans and a new T-shirt. Then she pulled a comb through her unruly hair, but finally gave up on her attempt to brush out the curls.

Surveying herself in the mirror, Amy sighed. It *would* have to be raining the first day back. Not a good sign. But things were bound to be better than last year. Maybe Kristen would be in some of her classes. It would be so wonderful to have someone to talk to—someone who understood about skating.

The first day at Walton Middle School was a bit chaotic. School counselors staffed tables in the cafeteria where they handed out class schedules. Amy waited almost thirty minutes before it was her turn. By the time she finally got her schedule, first period was nearly over.

First period: English. Second period: Social Studies. Third period: Math. Fourth period: Science. Fifth period: Art. Sixth period: P.E.

P.E.! Amy sighed. She couldn't see why she needed to take physical education. After all, she was planning to be skating a lot. At least she had art class. That should be fun.

It was a long day. Every teacher seemed determined to convince the students that this year was going to be really difficult. It sounded as though there would be lots of homework. Amy didn't really mind working hard, but she knew skating and baby-sitting were going to take extra time. At least that's what she was hoping.

It was disappointing to find that Kristen wasn't in any of her classes. By fourth period she was beginning to wonder if Kristen's family had decided to homeschool her again this year. Amy hoped that wasn't the case.

Long before the bell rang for lunch period, Amy's stomach was grumbling so loudly that she thought everyone in the school could hear it. When she finally got to the cafeteria, Amy chose a small table by herself. Most of the other kids had found their own friends to sit with anyway.

She had just taken a bite when someone came up behind her. "Hi, Amy. Is anyone sitting here?" Amy looked up to see Kristen standing there with a lunch tray. She looked like the perfect student, with a plaid jumper and matching short-sleeved sweater.

"You are," said Amy, her face brightening with a smile. She was glad to see a friend. She remembered that this was Kristen's first day of public school after homeschooling. "How's your first day going?"

Kristen made a face. "I think I got the most boring teachers in the school."

"You'll get used to it," said Amy. "At least there are people to talk to at school. Didn't you get lonely at home?"

"Sometimes. I think I'll like it here when I get to know everyone. Maybe you could introduce me around."

Amy looked a little embarrassed. "Well, I really don't know anyone very well myself. We only moved here last year. And my dad has been sick, so I really haven't gotten around to making friends."

"What's wrong with your dad?"

"He was in a really terrible car accident last year—he almost died. He's still in a wheelchair, but the doctor says he might be able to walk soon."

"Oh." Kristen seemed puzzled. "If your dad was hurt, why did you move?"

"Dad had to give up his business because he couldn't work," explained Amy. "Mom had to go back to work full-time; we moved here so my grandparents could help out with things at home."

"I'm sorry. Is that why you quit skating?"

Amy nodded. "Yeah. It was hard having to quit. I've really missed skating."

Kristen seems really concerned, thought Amy. No one else in Walton had ever been interested in any of her problems. It felt good to have someone care.

"Well, at least you're getting to skate again now," said Kristen. "And I hope your dad is able to walk soon. Is it okay if I pray for him?"

Amy didn't know what to say. "I guess so."

Just then the bell rang, signaling the end of lunch period. Kristen picked up her lunch tray. "Will you be at the skating rink today?"

"No," said Amy. "I can only come twice a week right now."

"Well, if I don't see you there, I'll see you at lunch tomorrow," said Kristen. She waved and headed to the cafeteria exit with her lunch tray. Amy waved back. She enjoyed having Kristen as a friend.

❈ ❈ ❈ ❈ ❈

Fifth period was art class. The teacher, Mrs. Ortega, seemed very nice, and Amy liked art. Their first assignment was to make a sketch of their favorite hobby. That was easy—Amy had certainly gotten lots of practice drawing her favorite subject.

"That's wonderful!" Mrs. Ortega was impressed when she saw Amy's picture. "You must like ice-skating."

Amy smiled. "I've been skating since I was little. I've got dozens of drawings at home."

Mrs. Ortega was interested. "The art club has been invited to do a media presentation of different sports in the front hall the next few weeks. Could you bring several of your best sketches for a skating display?"

"Sure." Amy was pleased that Mrs. Ortega liked her drawing.

"Amy, maybe you'd like to join the art club. The first meeting is next Thursday night at seven. We'd love to have you come."

"I don't know. I'll come if I can." Amy was flattered Mrs. Ortega asked her to join the art club. Even though Amy knew she would be busy this fall, perhaps she could squeeze in a few meetings.

❈ ❈ ❈ ❈ ❈

That afternoon, Amy went to the library for some books on baby-sitting and child development. She found two guidebooks for baby-sitters that looked like they might be helpful. If she was going to be baby-sitting, she had better learn something about it.

Later that evening, after she finished her homework and supper, Amy started reading the library books. Surprisingly enough, she found the books interesting. There were chapters about what children were like at different ages. Other chapters had tips for playing with the children and keeping them out of trouble. *This might be fun, after all,* she thought.

There was also a chapter on first aid, but Amy just skimmed through that one. After all, if she watched the children constantly and kept them busy, surely they wouldn't get hurt.

Amy read as much as she could. Before she knew it, it was time to turn out the lights and get into bed. But she couldn't sleep. There were too many things to think about. Amy lay awake for a long time making plans. Her life had suddenly become quite full.

❅ ❅ ❅ ❅ ❅

Amy was disappointed to find Kristen sitting with another girl at lunch the next day. Kristen and her friend were laughing and talking. They didn't seem to notice her. Amy tried to hide her disappointment as she began to look for another seat; then she heard Kristen calling her name.

"Amy, over here! Come and meet Shannon!" Amy turned and reluctantly made her way to Kristen's table. The girl with Kristen was tiny with short black hair and

Asian features. She looked up with a smile as Amy sat down. "Amy, this is Shannon Roberts," said Kristen. "And she's interested in skating!"

Anyone who likes skating must be okay, thought Amy. "Hi, Shannon," she said as she opened up her lunch and took out her sandwich and an apple. "Do you skate?"

"No," said Shannon. "But I'm hoping I can take lessons."

"Cool!" said Amy. "How did you two meet?"

"We're in the same social studies class," said Kristen. "Mrs. Tarlton put us in groups to work on a project, and Shannon was in my group. We're supposed to study Greek civilization and their Olympics."

"And just how much work did you get done?" teased Amy. "I don't think the ancient Greeks did much figure skating in their Olympics!"

"Not much!" admitted Kristen. "But I got to know Shannon! Can you come to the rink tomorrow afternoon, Amy? I'm going to get Shannon started skating."

"Mmm, I'm not sure, but I'll try. You'll like skating a lot, Shannon!"

"I hope so," said Shannon. "My mom said my little sister and I might be able to take lessons. My sister's only six, though."

"That's a good age to start," said Amy. "I started when I was seven, but I wish I could have started earlier. You know, most of the champions start really young, sometimes at three or four years old. How old were you when you started skating, Kristen?"

Kristen looked a little embarrassed. "I was five."

"No wonder you're so good!" said Amy.

"Well, you are looking pretty good yourself," said Kristen. "Especially considering you haven't been on the ice in a year!"

"It looks like I'm going to have a hard time catching up with you guys," said Shannon.

"Oh, don't worry!" added Kristen. "We'll make you a champion in no time! Won't we, Amy?"

"Sure thing!" Amy smiled. Now she had two new friends. Skating friends! Things were definitely looking up.

The three girls spent the rest of their lunch period talking and giggling as though they'd known each other for years. They hardly had enough time to eat their lunches. Before Amy knew it, it was time to go back to class.

"See ya later," she called out as the girls separated and headed for their next class. She was really looking forward to going skating with Kristen and Shannon.

❅ ❅ ❅ ❅ ❅

That evening after supper Amy asked her mother if it was all right if she went skating the next day. "Well, I'm not sure," said Mrs. Pederson. "I have to work late tomorrow, and your grandmother has an appointment to get her hair done. I was hoping you could start supper for me. Couldn't you wait until Thursday to go skating?"

"I have some new friends who are going to be at the rink tomorrow," said Amy. "Shannon's never skated before, and I promised to help her." Amy looked pleadingly at her mother. "Couldn't we make something tonight and heat it up tomorrow? Please?" It seemed ages since she had done something with friends.

Mrs. Pederson looked at her thoughtfully. "All right," she said. "I'll fix that new casserole I've been wanting to try. Joe can put it in when he gets home tomorrow."

"Thanks, Mom," said Amy, as she gave her mother a hug.

"Oh, I have some other news," said Mrs. Pederson. "I saw Mrs. Pulaski from across the street today. She asked if you were interested in baby-sitting for her on Saturday mornings while she works."

"Wow, another job!" said Amy. "Sure, I'll be glad to do it. How old are her kids?"

"Her little boy is four, and the girl is two, I think," said Mrs. Pederson. "Don't forget you're also baby-sitting the Thompson twins on Friday night. That's the first football game of the season."

"I know," said Amy. "I guess I'm going to be pretty busy."

A look of concern crossed her mother's face. "I hope you're not taking on too much. You've never really done this before, you know."

"I've read the books, Mom! It'll be a cinch."

"Well, I'll be home if you need any help," her mother said.

Amy went to her room to write Elizabeth about all the exciting changes in her life.

September 5

Dear Elizabeth,

You'll never believe this, but I met some girls in Walton who like skating! Kristen is really good. She and her brother used to skate at the rink in Richardson until the new rink opened. Shannon doesn't skate yet, but she's going to start taking lessons. We're going to meet at the rink tomorrow afternoon to skate together.

It will be fun to have some new skating friends, but they can never take your place. I still miss you and all the other kids at the rink in Glenview.

Your friend forever,
Amy

Amy had a hard time getting to sleep that night. She lay awake thinking about the money she was going to earn from baby-sitting. Maybe she could get back to a full training schedule. Amy considered how much it cost to have the ice time and the lessons she had had before her father's accident. Could she earn enough?

Five

The next afternoon after school Amy searched through some of her old skating dresses. Today she wanted to look like a real skater. And, she admitted to herself, she wanted to look good in front of Kristen. She decided on a black dress with red trim that had been her favorite.

Grandmother Pederson dropped Amy at the rink on the way to her hair appointment. "Be careful today!" she warned as she pulled up to the curb. Her grandmother thought ice-skating was dangerous.

"I will, Gram," said Amy. She got out of the car and headed into the rink. She wondered if Kristen and Shannon were there yet. *It is going to be fun to have someone to skate with again,* she thought.

Once inside, Amy quickly spotted Kristen and her brother. Kevin had his skates on and was battling starships on a game in the rink's arcade while he waited for the skating session to start. Kristen was showing

Shannon how to lace up a pair of rental skates. Shannon was wearing jeans and a sweatshirt.

Shannon's dark eyes were wide as she tried to follow Kristen's instructions.

"Hello, guys," said Amy as she plopped down on the bench beside the other girls and pulled out her own skates. "Looks like you're all ready, Shannon. Do you have gloves?"

Shannon held up a pair of hot pink gloves. "I have gloves," she said, "but I don't know if I'm ready. Are skates supposed to be this tight?"

"Oh, yes!" Kristen assured her. "If your skates are too loose, you won't even be able to stand up."

Shannon didn't really look convinced. "I'll take your word for it." She gave one last tug to her boots and stood up awkwardly. "I guess I'm as ready as I'll ever be!"

"Now, walk around for a few minutes," said Kristen. "That will help give you the feel of walking in skates."

"You can't teach anybody to skate!" Kevin had returned to pester Kristen and her friends.

"Kevin!" scolded Kristen. "Sorry, guys. This is my brother." She gave him a menacing look, which did absolutely no good. Amy and Shannon tried not to giggle; they knew Kristen was annoyed, but it was hard not to laugh at Kevin's teasing. He was cute, after all.

Kevin just grinned and winked at Shannon. He was clearly enjoying the attention. "Don't listen to her—she has no idea what she's doing!"

"Go skate, Kevin!" Kristen was getting exasperated.

Kevin pulled gloves out of his skate bag and headed for the ice. "Okay, but don't say I didn't warn you!"

Kristen turned back to her pupil. "Give it a try."

Shannon took a few tiny steps. "Hey, this isn't too bad! Can I walk like this on the ice?"

"Yes, at first," said Amy. "Take baby steps. Then, when you're ready, try gliding a little on each foot. Before you know it, you'll be skating!" She finished lacing her own skates. "Okay, let's go!"

The three girls started for the ice surface. Amy and Kristen got on first; then Shannon stepped timidly onto the ice, clutching the barrier.

"Eventually, you'll have to let go of the sides. Might as well do it now," said Amy.

"But I'll fall!" protested Shannon.

"That's our first lesson!" said Kristen. "We need to teach you how to fall!"

"Won't I do that anyway?" asked Shannon.

"All skaters have to know how to fall and get up again," said Kristen. "It's part of skating!"

"I thought when you got good at skating you didn't fall anymore," said Shannon.

"I wish!" said Amy. "But really, falling is no big deal. The important thing is not to fight it."

Just at that moment, Kevin zipped past at breakneck speed before crashing into the boards with a loud thump. The girls tried hard not to laugh, especially when he looked back at them with his red face matching his hair. Fortunately, he didn't seem to be hurt.

"Thank you for showing us how *not* to fall!" teased Kristen.

The girls had a great time together. Amy found that it was fun teaching a beginner; and Shannon was a fast learner. Before long she was gliding across the ice by herself, although a bit wobbly. And by the end of the session, Shannon was skating fairly confidently.

Amy hadn't had so much fun since she and Elizabeth had skated together in Glenview. And she was really pleased at her own progress. Although she still had a long way to go, she was beginning to feel more comfortable on the ice. Even her jumps were getting better, although she still couldn't land an axel.

While she practiced, Amy also watched Kristen. In a black crushed velvet practice dress with her auburn hair French-braided, Kristen looked very elegant. Amy couldn't help feeling some pangs of jealousy as she watched Kristen execute a perfect double toe loop*.

I used to be able to do that, Amy thought enviously. *I wonder if I will ever have to compete against Kristen.* She put that thought away quickly. She knew that she couldn't possibly compete right now. *Better get back to work or I won't be able to compete against anybody!*

All too soon, the skating session was over. It was time to clear the ice and let the big Zamboni* take over the rink. Shannon watched as the machine swept the ice, leaving behind a gleaming smooth surface.

"Wow! That looks cool!" Shannon said.

Amy and Kristen paid little attention. After years of

skating, they usually took the Zamboni for granted.

"Boy, am I tired!" said Shannon as the girls unlaced their skates. "And all I did was go round and round the rink! I can't imagine being able to do jumps and spins!"

"You will!" said Kristen. "You really did great today!"

Amy watched as Shannon pulled off the rental skates. Suddenly she had an idea. "Shannon, what size do you wear?" she asked.

"Four." All of Shannon was tiny, including her feet.

"I have some skates that might fit you," said Amy.

"That would be great!" Shannon looked at the ugly red rental skates she was wearing. "It would be cool to have real skates! Especially if they're white."

"They are, but actually, they're pretty scuffed up," admitted Amy. "But if they fit right, they'll help your skating. And you can polish them if you want to. You can try them on next time we come."

"Thanks," said Shannon. She smiled, and her dark eyes sparkled. "I can't wait to come again. See you at school tomorrow! Bye!" Shannon went on home, but Kristen and Amy were still taking care of their skating equipment. Carefully they wiped the blades dry and put terry cloth covers on them to protect them from moisture. Good skating boots and blades were expensive.

"C'mon, Kris," called Kevin from the door. "Let's go."

Kristen zipped her skate bag closed and stood up. "Would you like a ride home?" she offered.

"Thanks," said Amy, "but my mom is picking me up."

"How's your dad doing?" asked Kristen.

"The doctor says he's doing better. Thanks for asking."

"That's great," said Kristen. "I've been praying that God would help him to walk."

This was an awkward moment for Amy; she really wasn't sure what to say. Finally, she managed, "Thanks." She didn't know why, but talk about prayer always embarrassed her.

"We have a youth meeting on Saturday night at my church," said Kristen. "A lot of kids come, even kids who don't go to our church. Shannon is going to come this week. Would you like to come, too?"

"What kind of a meeting is it?" asked Amy. Her only experience with "church" had been the stuffy church services her family had occasionally attended before her father's accident. Amy thought it was usually boring.

"We play some games. Then we sing and afterward a speaker gives a short talk about something from the Bible. Then there are refreshments. It's a lot of fun."

Amy hesitated. "I'm not sure if I can go this time. I'll let you know."

"Okay. I hope you can come." Kristen waved as she headed out the door. "See ya tomorrow!"

Amy waved back. She wasn't sure if she wanted to go to a church meeting. *Religious people are sort of weird,* she thought. *And they probably aren't interested in skating. Of course, Kristen is a skater, but she's probably an exception.* Still, it was nice of Kristen to invite her. Maybe she would go sometime if she had nothing else to do, but not now. Amy knew her schedule was full. She didn't want to get involved in anything else.

Six

School and homework kept Amy so busy the rest of the week that she didn't have much time to think about skating. Before she knew it Friday night had arrived. Her first baby-sitting job! She reviewed her library books to get ready. She had already packed a bag with some small surprises for the little boys. The treats would be rewards for good behavior.

Amy was anxious to make a good impression, and she arrived fifteen minutes early at the Thompsons' house. Mrs. Thompson met her at the front door dressed in a knit top and matching slim pants. Her short brunette hair was perfectly styled.

"You must be Amy. I'm Mrs. Thompson. Joshua and Jarred are in the playroom. Why don't you go right in and get acquainted while I finish getting ready?"

Amy thought Mrs. Thompson looked quite ready for anything, but she followed her into a large room strewn with toys. Two blond, blue-eyed boys looked up from their building blocks as Amy walked in. Except for red overalls on one and blue on the other, they were absolutely identical. *They look like angels,* she thought.

"Hi, I'm Amy. Which one of you is Joshua, and which one is Jarred?"

"I'm Joshua," said one. He didn't smile, but looked her over curiously. "Do you want to play?"

"Sure," said Amy. "What are we playing?"

"I'm the commander of the army," said Joshua. "Everybody has to do what I say."

"Yes, sir!" said Amy, and she gave a quick salute. Joshua looked her over as if he were sizing up an opponent in battle.

"You go over there," he ordered, as he pointed to a spot in the corner. Amy went dutifully to the spot he assigned her and waited to see what would happen next. She wondered what the boys were planning. *They are so cute,* she thought. *This is going to be fun!*

Crash! Building blocks flew everywhere as Joshua knocked over the tall tower they had built. Then Jarred picked up a block and threw it at his brother. Before Amy knew it, she was dodging cardboard building blocks and trying to get out of the way.

"Hey, guys! Let's not throw things." Amy wondered how she was going to get the boys to stop.

"Boys, cut that out!" yelled Mrs. Thompson from the door. She grabbed one twin by the hand as she deftly stopped a flying block in midair. "Now, I expect you to behave yourselves this evening," she said to her sons. Then she turned to Amy. "I hope they'll be good. They've been a little wild today."

Amy smiled weakly and nodded. She was beginning to get a little nervous. Mrs. Thompson gave some quick instructions on snacks and bedtime and left her pager number before she hurried out the door.

Amy realized that she had better take charge quickly. "I brought a game to play," she said.

Joshua and Jarred looked interested. Amy went to her backpack and pulled out a ringtoss game. "Now, watch this," she said. Amy stood a few feet away and tossed a ring toward the target. "Oops, I missed. Oh, well, whoever gets the most rings over the target is the winner. Would you like to try?"

The boys were eager to play the game. Amy helped them toss the rings, but trouble broke out when Jarred made a couple of lucky shots.

"I win! I win!" he shouted.

"No, you don't!" yelled Joshua. He grabbed the rings off the target. "I don't wanna play this anymore."

"But I wanna play." Jarred ran after his brother, trying to get the rings. Before Amy could stop them, the two boys were wrestling on the floor, both screaming at the top of their lungs. *Now what do I do?* she thought.

Suddenly a shrill whistle arrested the boys. They immediately stopped fighting and looked around in surprise. Amy wore a satisfied grin. She would have to remember to thank Kurt for teaching her that trick.

"I have some surprises for you," Amy said sweetly.

The boys forgot all about the ringtoss and their fight. They stood still in their tracks. "What is it?" they asked.

"I won't tell you what it is," said Amy, "but if you will be very good the next two hours you will each get one."

"It's probably something dumb," said Joshua.

"No, it isn't dumb," she said. "But you won't find out if you're not good."

Joshua was quiet for a minute, considering. He looked at Jarred, then nodded. "We'll be good," he agreed.

"All right," said Amy. "No more fighting. Okay?"

"Okay." Both boys nodded. Amy sighed. She hoped this would work.

Things went smoothly for a while. Amy found some coloring books and crayons for them, but before long they were squabbling over the same color. It seemed every activity ended with a fight.

At last it was time for the boys to get ready for bed. Even though they didn't deserve them, Amy rewarded them with the candy she had brought for surprises. Then finally, she got them into bed. Exhausted, she sank gratefully into the big chair in the living room and turned on the television. Baby-sitting was hard work. *Oh, well, now I can relax,* Amy thought.

"I'm thirsty," called a little voice behind her chair. *Oh, no!* thought Amy, as she turned to see who was there. "You're supposed to be in bed," she scolded.

"But I'm thirsty," protested Joshua.

"All right, I'll get you a drink of water," said Amy.

"You get back in bed, and I'll bring it to you." She went into the kitchen and got a drink for both boys, just in case Jarred wanted a drink, too. But when she arrived in the bedroom, she found that Jarred was already asleep. "Shh," she whispered. "Don't wake Jarred."

Joshua drank his water. "Good night," said Amy. and returned to the living room.

For thirty minutes all was quiet. Amy was so tired she put her head down on the arm of the chair and dozed off. Suddenly a loud noise awakened her. Amy jumped up. For a minute she couldn't remember where she was. Then she realized a loud radio was playing somewhere. When she went to investigate, she noticed the light was on in the playroom. Both boys were there, and the radio was blaring at full blast.

"What are you doing?" Amy cried.

Joshua explained, "We want to play some more."

Frustrated, Amy herded the boys back into their beds. Then she stood guard outside their room, hushing them each time they made a sound. Whatever it took, she was determined to keep those troublesome boys in their beds until their parents came home.

❋ ❋ ❋ ❋ ❋

It was almost midnight when Amy arrived home. She was sure she couldn't be more tired if she had run a marathon race. "How were the twins?" asked Mrs. Pederson as she fixed Amy a snack.

"Mom, they were terrible," complained Amy. "They fought over everything the entire evening. And then they wouldn't go to bed."

"Really? They seem like such sweet little boys," Mrs. Pederson said.

"Looks can be deceiving," muttered Amy. She yawned sleepily. It was definitely time for bed.

Mrs. Pederson smiled. "Don't forget you promised to baby-sit for Mrs. Pulaski in the morning."

Amy groaned. Maybe baby-sitting wasn't such a good idea after all.

✳ ✳ ✳ ✳ ✳

When Amy arrived at the Pulaski home the next morning, the children were still in their pajamas. Sounds of Saturday morning cartoons blared forth from the television set, and toys decorated the living room floor. Mrs. Pulaski seemed very different from the capable Mrs. Thompson. Her long, brown hair was pulled back in a loose ponytail, and she was casually dressed in jeans and a big T-shirt.

"Just make yourself at home, Amy," said Mrs. Pulaski. "Tyler and Erin shouldn't be any trouble. They'll probably just watch TV all morning."

Amy settled into a comfortable chair in the living room along with the children. Four-year-old Tyler stared glassy-eyed at the television screen, oblivious to everything around him. Two-year-old Erin looked just like a little baby doll with her chubby pink cheeks and brown curls. Her thumb was in her mouth, and she seemed to be falling asleep. *At least this morning should be easier than last night,* Amy thought.

Everything went fine until Amy noticed that Erin seemed to be breathing fast. Her pink cheeks had become flaming red, and she was wiggling and moaning in her sleep. Amy felt her forehead. The child seemed awfully hot. *I hope she's not sick,* Amy thought anxiously.

At last Erin woke up with a whimper. Amy picked her up and held her, trying to think what to do. If Erin was sick, surely she should call Mrs. Pulaski. Did she leave an emergency number? Amy couldn't remember.

Suddenly Erin began making some strange sounds and then, *Oh, yuck!* The child vomited all over every-thing: herself, Amy, the sofa, and the floor. Then she started crying loudly. Amy sat holding her in disbelief. *Now what do I do?* she thought. Tyler's wails soon joined his sister's. "I want my mommy."

"Just a minute, Tyler." Amy tried to comfort both children while she tried to figure out the best way to clean up the mess. She was beginning to feel rather ill herself. At last she succeeded in getting to her feet with Erin in her arms. She carried the whimpering child to the bathroom as Tyler followed. Grabbing some towels off the racks, she wiped off Erin as best she could, then went to work on herself. The living room could wait.

After she had cleaned up the worst of the mess, Amy headed toward the telephone to find out if Mrs. Pulaski had left a number. She searched everywhere she could think of, but she couldn't find anything helpful. Vaguely, she remembered that a baby-sitter should *always* get emergency numbers, and she was angry at herself for forgetting something so important. *Maybe I shouldn't have skipped the chapter on emergencies,* she thought.

At least she could get her mother to help. Frantically, she dialed the number but was answered by a busy signal. Amy was getting desperate. The children were both wailing at the top of their lungs.

While she waited until she could get her mother on the phone, Amy did her best to take care of the children. She offered Tyler a snack and sat him in front of the television. Then she got a cool washcloth and put it on Erin's forehead, just as she remembered her own mother doing for her when she was sick.

Finally, she got her mother on the phone, and Mrs. Pederson came right over. While Amy played with Tyler, her mother bathed Erin, changed her clothes, and then sat and rocked the child.

"It's very difficult to know what to do for a sick child. You did the right thing by calling me and waiting for me to give the toddler a bath. I'm very proud of you," said Mrs. Pederson.

As soon as Amy got home, she went straight to bed and slept most of the afternoon. Baby-sitting hadn't been nearly as easy as she had expected.

Seven

"You should have come to the youth meeting with us," said Kristen when the three girls met in the school cafeteria on Monday. "It was really cool."

Amy had been so busy she had forgotten all about Kristen's youth meeting. "Well, maybe sometime I'll go with you guys," she said. She wasn't yet ready to commit to going. After all, she *did* have a pretty busy schedule.

"I'm glad I went," added Shannon. "I had a great time. We played games, and there were lots of goodies to eat. I'm going to go every week."

"I thought it was a religious meeting," teased Amy. Kristen smiled. "Well, we have fun, too, you know."

"I was so tired from baby-sitting I don't think I could have stayed awake for anything," Amy said. "You wouldn't believe those kids on Friday night. They were awful."

"Weren't you baby-sitting Coach Thompson's twins?" asked Kristen. "I've heard he's really strict with his football players."

"He must not be very strict at home. Those boys wouldn't behave at all." Amy frowned at the memory. "And I've got to keep them every Friday night—the whole football season."

"Maybe they'll pay you extra," put in Shannon.

"They *were* pretty generous," agreed Amy. "With what I made Friday night and Saturday morning, I'll be able to skate every afternoon this week."

"Oh, good," said Kristen. "You can help me put up with Kevin. Shannon, when are you skating again?"

Shannon's face lit up. "I'm starting lessons today. And so is my little sister."

"Great!" said Amy. "I'll bring those skates."

❄ ❄ ❄ ❄ ❄

Amy's old skates fit Shannon perfectly. She laced them up, then stared at them with shining eyes. "Now I feel like a real skater. Thanks, Amy."

Amy felt a warm glow. She could tell Shannon was really pleased. "Just be careful," she warned. "You'll have to get used to them. Don't try any triple axels for a while," she said with a grin.

"Very funny," said Shannon as she headed for the ice, her little sister Tiffany following close behind.

"My skates are prettier than yours, Shannon," said Tiffany, looking down at her brightly colored rental skates. "I like red."

Tiffany looked so cute. Even though she had never skated before, she was wearing a pink skating dress and warm tights. Her long dark hair hung in a pigtail down her back. She was all smiles as she wobbled on the ice. Shannon and Tiffany were going to have a lesson with one of the coaches that afternoon.

Kristen and her brother were already on the ice, although Kevin seemed to be doing more playing than practicing. Amy wondered if he ever took skating very seriously. In fact, she wondered if he took *anything* seriously.

Kristen was hard at work, as always, but she paused long enough to wave when she saw Amy step onto the ice.

It was time for Amy to get busy, too. She was determined to get back in shape. After she had warmed up by stroking around the rink, she went to work on jumps. First she performed several high waltz jumps*, taking off on her left foot, making a half turn in the air, and landing backward on her right foot.

Next Amy went through all of the single jumps: the salchow*, the toe loop*, the loop*, the flip*, and the lutz*. Although each jump is somewhat different, they all consist of a single complete turn in the air before landing on one foot. When a skater completes a jump properly, he or she is said to have "landed" the jump.

At last Amy was ready to try an axel, the most difficult of all the single jumps. She had worked for months to learn to do it properly. It was discouraging to have to start all over again, but she took a deep breath and started to work.

Taking off from a left forward edge*, Amy swung

her right leg forward and jumped into the air, pulling her arms close to her body to help in the rotation. Her left leg crossed over her right leg, then *Thud!* Amy crashed into the ice.

Slowly she picked herself up, brushing the ice from her tights. She needed to make one and a half rotations in the air to land on a backward edge, but she wasn't even making a full turn in the air. Again she tried, this time putting more force into her upward thrust. Once more she found herself sitting on the ice. Amy tried the jump several times, but although she increased the rotation, she still wasn't landing it right.

It was definitely time to take a break! Amy nursed her bruises and watched the other skaters for a while. Shannon was on the other side of the rink, listening intently to her instructor. Tiffany stood at the side, watching her sister. Kevin was nowhere to be seen. *Probably playing video games again,* she thought.

However, Kristen was in the center of the rink working hard on spins. Amy had never seen anyone so disciplined. She couldn't help admiring her new friend, but she wondered, *How can she be so perfect?*

Amy went back to practicing her jumps. Before she knew it, it was time to go home. She felt as though she had made no progress at all.

Then she felt a tug on her sweatshirt. "Did you see me skate?" She turned to see little Tiffany looking up at her.

"Yes, I saw you," said Amy with a smile. "You're doing great."

Tiffany grinned. "My teacher said I did good. One day I'm going to be a really good skater like you."

"You'll probably be even better than me," said Amy. *Especially if I can't get my axel,* she added to herself.

✳ ✳ ✳ ✳ ✳

All week Amy worked out at the rink. Gradually, she became more comfortable on the ice, and sometimes she almost felt good about her skating. Once she even landed a double salchow. But for some reason she still could not complete an axel.

In between practicing jumps and spins, Amy found time to help Shannon. It was the first time she had ever spent much time coaching another skater, and Amy was surprised to find that she really enjoyed it. Shannon was the perfect student. She seemed to grasp everything Amy told her; then she just did it. Already she was gliding confidently, and she had even begun to skate backward.

Amy soon found that she had a "little shadow" on the ice. Tiffany followed her around watching every move she made. Sometimes she wanted Amy to watch her skate, and Amy always clapped her gloved hands and told her what a wonderful skater she was. Tiffany was still pretty wobbly, but she didn't fall very often.

✳ ✳ ✳ ✳ ✳

By Thursday Amy decided that she was going to land an axel if it killed her! When she finished warming up, she began to work seriously on the axel. No spins or footwork* today.

Amy worked hard all afternoon. Over and over she fell as she put all her effort into the jump. Sometimes she came so close . . . but after nearly two hours she still had not managed to complete even one axel.

She felt like giving up. After taking a particularly bad fall, she found herself sitting on the ice for the thousandth time. This time she didn't get up right away; instead in frustration she sat on the ice. Looking up, she noticed Kristen setting up for an axel. But instead of rotating one and a half times, Kristen spun twice around before falling to the ice. *A double axel!* A double axel consists of two and a half rotations before landing on a backward edge. Kristen had failed to complete the rotations. Still, Amy couldn't help feeling some twinges of jealousy as she watched.

Slowly, Amy got up and made her way off the ice. Somehow she didn't feel like skating anymore that day. Sullenly, she pulled off her skates and put them away in her skate bag. Of course, Kristen had not had to take a year off the ice as Amy had, and Kristen skated every day. And Amy knew that her friend not only skated in the public sessions, but also in the early morning private sessions—sometimes called freestyles.

Amy also knew that Kristen was taking lessons with Elena Grischenko, the famous Ukrainian coach who was the new skating director at the rink. Coach Grischenko had coached several skaters to the championship level. With top coaching like that, it was no wonder that Kristen was such a good skater.

It just isn't fair. Amy dabbed at a tear that was escaping down her cheek. She knew that she shouldn't be feeling sorry for herself, but she just couldn't help it. *I would be working on a double axel right now if I hadn't had to stop skating,* she told herself. Instead, here she was trying to finance her own skating by baby-sitting naughty kids. No lessons, old skates, and not enough time to practice.

In the midst of her "pity party," Amy looked up to see Shannon practicing crossovers*. Amy was amazed. She had never seen anyone progress so fast. Although Shannon was doing only very basic moves, she was skating smoothly and confidently. *Before long even Shannon will be outskating me. I wish I hadn't given her my old skates.*

Amy didn't feel like talking to anyone. She called Grandmother Pederson and asked her to come pick her up. Then she packed up her skates and went outside to wait. She hoped that Shannon and Kristen wouldn't notice that she was gone.

❄ ✳ ❄ ✳ ❄

"Do you mind if I don't help with the dishes tonight, Mom?" Amy asked after supper that evening. "I've got a lot of homework to get done before the art club meeting."

Her mother began clearing the table. "All right, Amy. But are you sure you're up to a meeting tonight? You seem tired."

"I'm fine," Amy lied. "I've just been working hard at the rink this week." She slipped out of the dining room before her mother could say anything else. She was glad she had a good excuse to be alone.

However, before she could get started on her homework, she heard the phone ring.

"Telephone, Amy!" called her mother a few seconds later.

"I'll get it in here, Mom." Amy went to the phone in her parents' room.

"Amy, this is Kristen."

"Oh, hi." Amy hoped she sounded friendlier than she felt.

"What happened to you this afternoon? Shannon and I looked for you after skating. You didn't get hurt, did you? I saw you take a pretty bad fall."

"Oh, no, everything's fine," Amy lied. "I just had a lot of homework, so I left a little early, that's all."

"Oh, well, I'm glad you're okay." Kristen sounded unconvinced. "Are you going to skate tomorrow?"

"I'm not sure. I have to baby-sit tomorrow night."

"My mom would be glad to give you a ride home," offered Kristen.

"Well, I'll let you know." Amy paused as she searched for an excuse. "Mrs. Thompson said she might need me early."

"Well, I hope you can come. Oh, before I forget, do you think you could come to the youth meeting on Saturday? I know you've got a lot to do, but this week is special. Bob Crandall is speaking."

"The hockey player Bob Crandall?" He was one of the top players in pro hockey.

"Yes," said Kristen. "Our youth director knew him from school, and Crandall agreed to come to our meeting while he's in town. I can't wait to hear him. Do you think you could come?"

Amy stalled, trying to think up an excuse. "Maybe, if I'm not too tired." Right now she wasn't interested in religious hockey players. "Listen, Kristen, I really have to go. If I don't get this homework done, I'm going to be in big trouble in history class tomorrow."

"Oh, okay." Kristen sounded disappointed. "Well, I'll see you at lunch tomorrow."

"Sure thing." Amy hung up feeling guilty. She knew she hadn't been very friendly, but she didn't feel like talking to anyone right now, especially Kristen.

Eight

What have I gotten myself into now? As Amy dialed her locker combination the next morning, she thought about what had happened at the art club meeting the night before. Amy couldn't believe she had been elected vice president of the club. She pulled the books she needed from her locker and headed down the hall. There were still a few minutes left before class, and Amy wanted to look at the "Sports in Art" display in the main hall. Putting up the display had taken most of the club's meeting, and she had to leave before it was finished.

She found Shannon and Kristen looking at the display. "Wow, Amy, are these your pictures?" asked Shannon. "I can't believe you can draw like that!"

"Thanks," said Amy. "But I really can't draw anything but skaters!"

"I'll bet you could if you tried," said Kristen. "But the skating pictures are great. Thank goodness it's not all football and basketball."

Amy nodded. Kristen was right; most of the display centered around the school's teams. "I know. Lance Anderson is the best artist in the school, and those are his two favorite sports."

"Speaking of sports," said Kristen, "Shannon learned a two-foot spin* yesterday."

"Wow! And you just started skating! Before you know it, you'll be beating us in competitions."

Shannon looked embarrassed. "I'll never be as good as you guys."

"Just wait," said Kristen. "With our help, you'll be doing great stuff real fast!"

With the excitement of the art club meeting, Amy had almost forgotten about the incident on the ice yesterday. Now she remembered. Shannon and Kristen didn't seem to notice that Amy had suddenly become quiet. Amy wished she felt as cheerful as they did. But then, everything was going fine for them.

Suddenly, Shannon interrupted her thoughts. "Are you coming to the meeting tomorrow night, Amy?" she asked. "I can't wait to see what Bob Crandall is really like. I've never met a famous person before. I wonder if we can get his autograph." Shannon seemed so excited, it took Amy by surprise.

"I don't know—" began Amy.

"You have to come," urged Shannon. "Doesn't she, Kristen?"

"I wish you could," said Kristen. She looked at Amy hopefully.

Amy felt cornered. Her friends seemed to really want her to go. "Well, if my mom will let me," she said.

"Oh, good, we'll pick you up tomorrow night at 6:30," said Kristen.

But before Amy could answer, the five-minute warning bell sounded, and the girls had to head for class. "See you at lunch," said Kristen. There wasn't time to say anything else.

Amy wondered why she had given in so easily. With skating, school, baby-sitting, and the art club meetings, Amy was finding herself busier than ever before. Going to a church meeting was the last thing she wanted to do right now.

❄ ❄ ❄ ❄ ❄

As she was getting dressed to go to the youth meeting on Saturday night, Amy seriously considered backing out of her promise. Even though her weekend baby-sitting jobs had gone more smoothly this time, she was still pretty tired. Amy sighed as she brushed her hair into a ponytail. All she really wanted to do was crash in front of the TV.

But somehow, Amy couldn't bring herself to call Kristen and tell her she wasn't coming. She knew that her friends would continue asking until she came at least once. Maybe it was better to just get it over with.

❄ ❄ ❄ ❄ ❄

The youth meeting took place in the church gym. There were about twenty-five kids there, some of whom she recognized from the middle school. A few were high school age. Amy was glad to be with Kristen and Shannon, since she didn't really know anyone else. Kevin had come with them, but he was hanging around with some of the guys from school.

Amy looked at the refreshment table, loaded with all kinds of goodies. "When do we get to eat?"

"They make us sit through the meeting first," answered Shannon.

"Of course, there are some veggies and dip for us serious skaters," teased Kristen.

"Speak for yourself," said Amy. "I'm going for those brownies with fudge frosting!"

A slightly balding young man called the meeting to order. "That's Mike, our youth minister," Kristen whispered to Amy. Mike lined everyone up to play some games. To her surprise, Bob Crandall joined in and insisted that everyone call him "Bob." Amy had considered sitting out. But before she knew it, she had gotten involved in trying to guess some of the riddles. To her surprise, she found herself having fun. When the games were finished, Mike led them in a few songs. Since Amy didn't know any of them, she watched the others sing. Even Kevin was singing along with everyone else. It all seemed a bit silly to her.

When Bob Crandall finally got up to speak, everyone hushed. Many of the kids had come just to hear him.

Amy found that she couldn't help listening, whether she wanted to or not.

He started off by telling the group about his early life. He had come from a home where money was not available for sports. Fascinated, Amy listened while he told of running errands to earn money to pay for his equipment and working for his coaches to pay their fees. *Just like me!* she thought. Bob said sometimes he had been so discouraged he felt like quitting. "Some of the other players seemed to have it so easy!" he said. "Once in a while I wondered if it was worth it to have to work so hard. There was one time I nearly quit for good. But I loved playing hockey so much I had to come back."

Amy blinked away tears. She knew what it was like to want something so badly you were willing to do anything.

Bob went on to talk about getting a scholarship to play for a college team. From there he went on to pro hockey. "Hockey was my life. For the first time, I didn't have to worry about money. I was having a good time. I did a lot of things I'm not very proud of. Life was pretty good, and I had what I had always wanted. I didn't care about anything else.

"Then Jim Edwards, a friend of mine, got hit in a game. He was paralyzed from the waist down. Jim will never walk again. But when I went to see him in the hospital, all he could talk about was how lucky he was. I couldn't believe it. 'Bob,' he said, 'there's more to life than hockey. I still have God, and I know He has something more for me to do in this life, even if I'm paralyzed. What if it happens to you, Bob?'

"Right there I got to thinking. Hockey is a rough game, and I could be out in a minute, just like Jim. But Jim didn't give up. He can't play hockey anymore; he can't even walk. But he didn't stop living. He is still serving his God. Jim taught me that I needed Jesus in my life. Jesus loved me so much that He died for me.

"It took a long time, but one day I decided I wanted what Jim had. I asked Jesus to save me and be the Lord of my life. I started reading my Bible. One of the verses I found was this one. It's 1 Corinthians 9:24–25. 'You know that in a race all the runners run. But only one gets the prize. So run like that. Run to win! All those who compete in the games use strict training. They do this so that they can win a crown. That crown is an earthly thing that lasts only a short time. But our crown will continue forever.'

"It's great to win, isn't it? It's a high to win a hockey game. But in a few years there will be all new players and new teams. Sure, some people may remember my name. They may even remember some of the games I played in. But it won't really matter anymore.

"Jim taught me that there is more than one game going on in my life. And if I win at the wrong game, if I win at hockey but lose the game that really matters, I might as well not have won at all."

❋ ❋ ❋ ❋ ❋

After the meeting, the three girls sat on the steps outside the gym eating cookies. Amy shivered a little. It was an unusually cool night for September in Texas.

"What did you guys think about Bob Crandall?" asked Kristen.

"He was really cool," said Shannon. "I never knew he was a Christian. He gave me a lot to think about."

Amy was quiet. She didn't really know what she thought. Although she had gone to church occasionally, she had never really paid much attention. She assumed that church was to teach you to be good, and she figured that she was pretty good already. But Bob Crandall seemed really sincere.

Kristen looked at Amy. "What did you think, Amy?"

"Well, he was interesting." Just then Kristen's mother drove up, and the discussion ended. Amy was relieved she didn't need to say any more.

But that night Amy thought a lot about what Bob had said. This idea of serving Jesus was new to her. Maybe she would read the Bible to find out a little more. She searched her room and found her old Bible, a New Testament she had been given when she was a baby. As she flipped through the little book, Amy wondered if she could find the verse about "running a race" and "winning a prize." Skating wasn't exactly a race, but more than anything else in her life, it was something in which she was determined to win.

Nine

It was hard to believe it was already October. The long, hot summer was finally over, and the weather was getting cooler at last. Amy was very busy—much too busy to think about Bible verses.

But things were looking better these days. Baby-sitting was still a challenge, but Amy had learned how to handle Joshua and Jarred. Mr. Pederson had begun learning to use a walker. And Mom had been promoted in her job, with a small raise in salary.

Even school was going well this year. It helped to have friends. Kristen and Shannon were great; and through the art club Amy had gotten acquainted with some of the other kids at school.

Life was definitely getting better. It started with her axel. After several weeks, Amy finally landed it one afternoon.

When she arrived at the rink that day, Amy found Kristen and Shannon already on the ice. Shannon was really making rapid progress in skating. After only a few weeks she was already doing some simple jumps.

Kristen was using the time to work on her double axel. Amy watched enviously for a few minutes before she put on her skates. As hard as she tried, she couldn't help being jealous. She knew it would be quite awhile before she was ready to work on her double axel.

Amy felt a tug on her sweatshirt. "Watch me, Amy!" said Tiffany, Shannon's little sister. She looked up at Amy with huge dark eyes.

"Okay, Tiff," said Amy. "I'm watching. Go show me what you can do."

Tiffany smiled and trotted onto the ice. Amy watched as the little girl skated in a circle, her face twisted in concentration. Slowly, she crossed one foot over the other. She looked up to make sure that Amy was watching, then landed suddenly on her rear end. But she quickly scrambled back to her feet and started again. Tiffany was progressing quickly.

Amy put on her skates and joined her friends on the ice. By this time the session had become more crowded. Amy worked on spins, since spins don't take as much room as jumps. It was a frustrating session, and she spent most of it dodging beginning skaters. She was thinking of leaving early, when she realized that much of the crowd had left. Amy looked around and decided to spend a few minutes working on her axel before she took off her skates.

To her surprise she found that her axel felt better than usual. The first time she tried she came close to landing it. Amy began to get excited. Maybe she could land it today! Over and over she tried. After several falls, she was almost ready to give up, but she decided to try once more. To her surprise, this time she came down on one foot, a little shakily but still a decent landing. Amy couldn't believe it.

"Amy, you landed your axel!" She looked up to see Kristen smiling at her. "That's great!"

Amy was so thrilled she could hardly answer. "It's about time! I was almost ready to give up."

Just then Shannon joined them. "Hey, what's going on?"

"Amy landed her axel!" said Kristen.

"Oh, Amy, that's great!" said Shannon. "I know how hard you've been working on that jump."

"I think it's time for a celebration," said Kristen. "Guess what? I have more good news."

"Nothing could be better than this," said Amy.

"Listen, don't tell anyone yet," said Kristen. She lowered her voice. "My coach told me there's going to be a competition at this rink."

"Really? When?" Amy's face lit up with interest. She had always loved competing; she would like to add to the collection of ribbons and medals she'd won. It was exciting to her to work on a program set to music and then actually perform it.

"In January, I think."

"Oh, Shannon, this will be your first competition!"

"Not me! I couldn't!"

Both Amy and Kristen looked at her in surprise. "Why not?" they asked.

"I'm not ready for anything like that," Shannon protested. "I just started skating. Most of the kids my age are doing double jumps."

"There are lots of different levels," explained Kristen. "You'll only be competing against kids who are skating at your level."

Shannon looked doubtful. "Come on, you can do it," encouraged Amy.

"I'll think about it," said Shannon. "I'm not sure if I can get ready in time."

Amy put her hands on her hips and looked at Kristen. "We'll just have to talk her into it."

Kristen nodded. "You'll see, it'll be fun. But we'd better get back to work, or none of us will be ready." She skated away and began to work on spins.

Shannon sighed. "If I'm going to have to compete, I guess I'd better get to work, too. See ya later, Amy."

But Amy found it difficult to concentrate on her skating. She was really excited about the prospect of a competition, but at the same time she realized there were going to be some problems. Competing cost money. There would be an entry fee, and she would have to have a coach, a program, and music. Finances were still tight at home. Even though Mom had gotten a raise and Dad was working, there were so many medical bills. Amy's baby-sitting was just barely paying for her skating time.

At least she already had a costume—there were one or two competition dresses at home that would probably still fit her. She would wear the blue one; she had always liked it best. And her skates. She'd need new skates; these were beginning to hurt her feet. But mostly, Amy wondered whether she could get her skating back to competition level. She had only just gotten her axel back. If she had to pay for lessons, she would not be able to afford as much time on the ice. Even if she began working on a program right away, would she be able to get ready in time?

And would she have to compete against Kristen? Amy wasn't sure she liked the thought. Of course, she had often competed against friends in the past. But this time it was different. She wasn't exactly sure why, but Amy felt uncomfortable about having to compete against her new friend. She glanced at Kristen and saw her attempt another double axel. This time Kristen almost landed it, but ended up falling again. As much as Amy hated to admit it, she knew she was secretly glad Kristen hadn't succeeded in landing the jump yet. But she also knew that if she had to compete against her friend right now, Kristen would be the clear winner.

❄ ❄ ❄ ❄ ❄

"Shannon, you've got to decide on music for the competition," announced Kristen at lunch the next day. "Any ideas?"

Shannon looked surprised. "I thought your coach picked your music."

"Some of them do," said Amy. "But my coach in Virginia always let me pick my own. He said I would skate better if I had music I really liked."

70

"What are you going to skate to, Amy?" Kristen asked.

"I'm thinking about something from *The Sound of Music*," said Amy. "I've got a blue costume that would be perfect, and I like to skate to something fun. What about you, Kristen?"

Kristen thought for a moment. "Probably something classical."

Amy turned to Shannon. "Okay, it's your turn. What kind of music do you like?"

"I have no idea. I'm not even sure I want to compete," admitted Shannon.

"You'll do great," Amy assured her. "It will be fun."

"Fun? Skating in front of judges and getting all nervous is fun?"

Amy and Kristen looked at each other and grinned. "Don't ask me why, but it is," said Kristen.

Amy laughed and then added, "Skaters are just strange people!"

❋ ❋ ❋ ❋ ❋

Amy decided to talk to her mother about the competition that evening after supper. "Mom, there's going to be a competition at the rink." Amy put a plate in the dishwasher, then looked up hopefully at her mother. "Do you think I could do it?"

"When is it?" Mrs. Pederson grabbed the dishcloth and began wiping the table.

"In January."

"Do you think you could get a program ready in time?"

Amy nodded. "I'm sure I can; but there will be an entry fee."

Her mother looked at her and sighed. "You've worked so hard to pay for your skate time. Go ahead and enter the competition. We'll find a way to pay the entry fee."

Amy gave her mother a hug. "Thanks, Mom. I may not be able to come up with a winning performance, but I really miss competing."

Mrs. Pederson put her arm around Amy and said, "You're always a winner to us, you know. I'm proud of you for trying."

It was great to have her mother's support. But Amy knew that she wouldn't really be happy with anything but a first-place medal. And somehow she was determined to get it.

✳ ✳ ✳ ✳ ✳

Shannon wasn't very excited about the prospect of competing, but her coach had practically insisted that she give it a try. Tiffany was competing, too, in the six-year-old group. She was thrilled. "I'm going to win," she assured the older girls. Then she skated off in a sort of victory dance. If it were possible to "prance" in skates, Tiffany was doing it. Shannon and her friends laughed as they watched her antics.

Even Kevin was going to enter the competition. "I have no choice," he told the girls. "Somebody around here has got to show how this is done."

"Well, it won't be you!" Kristen assured him. "You hardly ever practice."

"That's because I don't have to," he said, wiping ice from his blade and flicking it onto his sister. "I'm already the best."

Kristen looked as though she intended to inflict bodily harm.

"Never mind, Kristen," said Amy, stepping between the two. "We'll do our bragging on the ice."

It was fun to be deciding on a program and music again. Amy enjoyed searching for her music. There must be a beginning, an ending, and both fast and slow parts in order to show what the skater can do. Then the music has to be edited to fit the routine and the time length of the performance. It was a relief to Amy when Kristen offered to "cut" Amy's music for her on her family's stereo system.

Amy could plan her own skating routine. She knew what moves were required and felt she could put together a good program. Even so, she would still need a few sessions with a coach to help her smooth out the rough edges of her program and help her during the competition.

But would her skating be ready in time?

Ten

November 12

Dear Elizabeth,

Our new rink is having its first competition in January. I'm so excited. I've almost got my program worked out. I'm hoping to have some lessons with Elena Grischenko, the famous coach. But I'm having a hard time coming up with the money. Football season is over, so there goes my Friday night baby-sitting job. Luckily, I'm still baby-sitting Tyler and Erin on Saturday mornings, and I've had a few other jobs. Oh, well, if I have to, I'll coach myself!

Love,
Amy

Amy spent a lot of time the next few weeks helping Shannon prepare for the competition. Shannon had decided to skate to music from *Star Wars,* and her coach had worked out a program for her. Even though she was still nervous about competing, she was beginning to get excited. Amy was almost as anxious for Shannon to do well as she was for herself. She dug out all her old competition dresses for her to try on.

"I'm so glad you are letting me borrow a costume," said Shannon.

"That's one of the really cool things about skating. Almost everyone borrows costumes," Amy said, then laughed. "My mother says I never throw anything away and someday I'll have so much skating stuff I won't be able to get into my room."

Shannon's first choice was a pretty pink dress.

"Oh, Amy, this is gorgeous," said Shannon when she tried it on. The dress had a chiffon skirt and sleeves and was trimmed around the neck and cuffs with a band of sequins and pearls. "I feel like I could win the Olympics with this dress."

"It looks great on you," agreed Amy. "I can't believe it fits. I wore that dress to a competition two years ago."

"Sometimes I think I'm never going to grow," Shannon said. "You know, I'm adopted." Then rolling her eyes she added, "When I say something about wanting to get taller my dad laughs and says it's one of the 'great mysteries of my life' how tall I might grow—or *not* grow! Parents!"

Amy shrugged. "A lot of famous skaters have been short. Anyway, the dress is perfect, although maybe it's a little fancy for your routine. But it doesn't really matter. I'm glad I had a dress that fit you."

"I love it. I'll have to practice really hard to live up to this dress. I'm so nervous."

"You'll do great," Amy assured her. "Everybody's nervous for their first competition." She laughed. "Come to think of it, everybody's nervous for *every* competition."

"I'm so nervous," said Shannon, "that this may be my *only* competition."

❊ ❊ ❊ ❊ ❊

It was Friday afternoon, and the three girls were unlacing their skates after practice. "Let's all go to the Dairy Haven for ice cream," Shannon suggested. "Since Tiffany didn't come today, I don't have to go right home."

"I'll have to call my mom," said Amy, "but I probably can. I don't have to baby-sit tonight. How about you, Kristen?"

"I'd love to. I'll call and see if it's okay."

Half an hour later the three girls were sitting in a booth eating Avalanches, special milk shakes with bits of candy mixed in. "Mmm, mine is delicious." Kristen closed her eyes as she savored the treat.

Amy took a bite of hers. "We didn't have Dairy Havens in Virginia."

"Boy, were you guys missing out," Shannon teased.

"I'm glad I live in Texas. Aren't you glad you moved here?"

Amy didn't smile. "I used to hate it here."

Shannon and Kristen looked surprised.

"Do you still hate it?" asked Kristen.

"No, I don't hate it anymore. It's a lot better now that I have two great friends." Amy smiled at Kristen and Shannon. "But sometimes I still miss Glenview."

"I guess it would be pretty tough to move across the country," said Shannon. "I've lived in Walton all my life. I wouldn't want to move."

"When I was little, my family lived in Oklahoma," said Kristen. "I started skating there. When we first moved here, I was miserable. I hated everything about it."

"I didn't know that," said Amy. "How long have you lived in Walton?"

"Almost four years," said Kristen. "For the first three years we were homeschooled because it was so far to the nearest skating rink. I really liked homeschooling, but I had a hard time making friends since I wasn't in regular school. It was easier for Kevin. He played soccer here in Walton, and he made a lot of friends that way. But the only kids I ever saw were at the skating rink in Richardson. I was really lonely."

Amy listened sympathetically. "Boy, I know just what that's like."

Kristen went on. "That's when we started going to church."

"Church?" asked Amy.

"Yes," said Kristen. "It's really important to me. I didn't feel like I had anything in common with the other kids. They were all busy with school, and I felt left out. I really wanted a friend. One day the pastor said that Jesus was the best friend we could ever have. I thought about that for a long time. Later he said that Jesus loved me so much He died for my sins."

Amy looked a little embarrassed. This discussion was getting a little too personal, and she wasn't really sure what to say.

It was quiet for a minute as the girls finished up the last of their Avalanches. Then Amy looked at her watch. "Uh-oh! My mom will be here any minute. I'd better go watch for her. See you guys next week, okay?" Amy headed for the door. As she walked outside, she thought about what Kristen had said. *Is that why she's so different?* Amy wondered.

❄ ❄ ❄ ❄ ❄

On Monday afternoon, Amy went to the rink and took out her skates. Figure skating boots are supposed to fit very closely, but lately hers had felt tighter than usual. As much as Amy liked to skate she dreaded putting on those skates. Amy studied her feet. Her toes were bruised, and she had "water blisters" on her feet. But new skates were out of the question. Amy tugged on her boots. She tied her laces and stood up. *Maybe my feet are just a little swollen today,* she thought. She walked around on the floor for a few minutes, hoping that the boots would become more comfortable. They didn't. Then she took off her skates and started over, lacing them a bit more loosely. Nothing helped.

Amy realized what had happened. Her feet had grown. For a long time, she just sat there taking in what this would mean. She would have to have new skates.

Skates are the most important equipment a figure skater has. Without proper, well-fitting boots and special blades it is impossible to perform the difficult jumps, spins, and turns that make up the sport. And good skating boots are very expensive. Before Mr. Pederson's accident, buying new boots and blades had never been a problem. When it was time for the next pair, Amy's mother simply ordered them.

Things were different now. There was no money in the family budget to buy skating equipment. And the competition was only two months away. Amy surveyed the long line of rental skates. She wished she could turn a pair of them into advanced figure skates. But she knew she could never do complicated footwork in rental skates.

Amy relaced her boots once more. She would just have to put up with boots that hurt her feet. She had no choice.

Eleven

December 10

Dear Elizabeth,

I can't believe it's almost Christmas. It feels like spring outside. Kurt doesn't mind—he hopes it will be warm on Christmas so that he can try out his new Rollerblades.

I finally had a lesson with Coach Grischenko. She's really tough, but I like her. Paying for lessons means I can only skate three days a week, though. Even worse, my skates are too small! Actually, it's amazing that I've been able to wear them so long, but I don't know how I'm going to get new skates. I'm hoping I can at least get through the competition.

Love,
Amy

"More speed, Amy!" Coach Grischenko called as Amy flew over the ice to the music. Amy concentrated on performing the difficult footwork. Then she launched into her final move—a double toe-single loop combination jump*. The double toe was pretty strong, but the single loop was a little shaky. Amy struck her final pose and glanced over at her coach for approval. However, Coach Grischenko was not smiling.

"Sloppy work!" Coach Grischenko shook her head and launched into a critique of Amy's skating. Her thick Ukrainian accent sharply punctuated every word. Elena Grischenko was a strict coach, but Amy could already see an improvement in her competition program. Even though she had had to give up some of her practice sessions to pay for the lessons, she knew it was definitely worth the sacrifice.

"Now again!" Coach Grischenko turned to start the tape over. Amy took her starting position and began her program once more, trying to incorporate everything Coach Grischenko had told her to do. Amy's routine was fast-moving and entertaining, with a lot of dance steps. She loved performing it.

When her lesson was finished, Amy watched while Kristen ran through her own program. She had to admit her routine looked really good. Kristen was a beautiful classical skater. However, Amy felt sure the judges would prefer a more show-style theme.

There were a few more minutes left in the session, but Amy decided to take her skates off. She was tired, and her skates were becoming more and more uncomfortable. Often, when she took them off, her feet hurt so badly that she could hardly walk. Amy knew this was not good for her feet, but she couldn't help it. She was determined to skate in the competition, so she would just have to put up with the pain.

And after the competition, then what? Amy pushed the thought out of her mind. She would worry about that when the time came. Somehow she would find a way to get new skates.

In spite of the problems with her skates, things were really going pretty well these days. For the first time since she had moved to Walton, Amy was enjoying school. She had even made some new friends, several in the art club. In addition to her duties as vice president, Amy had also volunteered to help decorate for the Christmas party. Several times she had missed lunch with her friends to meet with the planning committee.

The Saturday morning baby-sitting job had ended, but Amy almost always had a job every Friday and Saturday night. Although Kristen and Shannon had invited her several times, she hadn't been back to the youth meeting since the night Bob Crandall spoke. Even when she didn't have to baby-sit, she needed most of the weekend to catch up on schoolwork.

All in all, things were going pretty well, if only she could manage to wear her skates a few more weeks.

❉ ❉ ❉ ❉ ❉

Amy arrived home early one afternoon to find that her father was already there. She was surprised to see him since he usually rode home with her mother.

Mr. Pederson was sitting in his wheelchair in the den. He seemed preoccupied; at first he didn't seem to even notice Amy when she came in. The room was dark; Amy wondered why he was sitting there doing nothing. "Hi, Dad," said Amy, as she threw her books on the dining room table. "You're home early."

It was a question as much as a statement. "Oh, they gave me the afternoon off," he answered, smiling.

Amy couldn't help noticing that he looked especially tired. She wondered if he was ill. "Are you okay, Dad?" she asked anxiously.

"Yes, I'm fine." He smiled. "I guess we need to work on dinner." He turned and started wheeling his way toward the kitchen.

Amy was not reassured. Somehow she knew something was wrong, but she followed him into the kitchen and began to pull out utensils to work on supper.

Before long, the two of them were laughing and having a good time as they started the spaghetti sauce. Mr. Pederson stationed himself at the kitchen table, putting together a salad. Amy enjoyed being with her father, although she didn't often have time alone with him. For the moment, she forgot about her concerns.

❀ ❀ ❀ ❀ ❀

Later that evening, the family gathered around the table for the dinner Amy and her father had prepared.

"Boy, this sure looks good," said Joe as he heaped spaghetti on his plate. Joe loved Italian food.

"Amy made it," volunteered Kurt, who had arrived home earlier than Joe.

"Oh, no, maybe I'm not hungry," Joe teased, then proceeded to dig in.

"I have to admit, Amy," her mother said, "I sort of enjoy the nights you don't skate. It helps so much to have dinner started when I get home from work."

"Besides, she's a good cook," said Mr. Pederson.

"Yeah, Amy, I was only teasing a minute ago, you know," said Joe. "This *is* really good. I'm hungry, too. We worked hard at basketball practice this afternoon."

"Thanks," said Amy as she helped herself to the salad. The praise from her family made her feel a little guilty. With her busy schedule, Amy knew she didn't help out as much as she should.

Amy had almost forgotten her worries about her father. Although he was laughing and joking with the rest of the family, he seemed very tired and old. Amy wondered again if he was sick.

When they finished eating, Mr. Pederson said, "I have something important to say." Amy noticed her mother suddenly looked sober.

"I'm going to have to find another job."

The family was silent for a few moments while the news sank in.

"But it's almost Christmas," protested Kurt. "They can't fire you at Christmas."

"They just don't need me right now, Kurt," said his father. "It can't be helped."

"Don't worry, Dad," said Joe. "There'll be something soon."

Amy didn't say anything. Deep down, she knew her main concern should be her family. But right now all she could think about was her skates. With her father out of work, money at home would be tighter than ever. Amy realized there would be no way in the world her family could help her get new skates now.

❄ ❄ ❄ ❄ ❄

The news that her father had lost his job put an end to Amy's Christmas spirit. Her mother got out the Christmas decorations and played Christmas music on the stereo, but Amy couldn't find much to be joyful about. It seemed so unfair for her dad to lose his job now, just when she thought things were starting to get better.

Joe and Kurt didn't seem concerned. They were confident that Dad would find more work pretty soon. And the loss of income didn't affect them very much anyway. They still had their sports.

Amy knew that there wouldn't be many presents this Christmas. She didn't really care about that. She could live without presents. But she was sure she couldn't live without skating.

At least she didn't have to stop skating yet. With

Christmas shopping in full swing, Amy had many baby-sitting opportunities. She was earning enough to skate and pay for her lessons with Coach Grischenko as well.

❄ ❄ ❄ ❄ ❄

December weather in northeastern Texas can be fickle. One day it may be warm and sunny. The next day the howling wind may bring biting cold with it. This year the weather was cooperating beautifully with the Christmas season. One mid-December day snowflakes fell fast and thick on Walton Middle School. Even though they melted as soon as they touched the ground, the sight of snow put almost everyone into the Christmas spirit.

Amy watched out the window as students, excused from classes for a few minutes, ran outside to catch snowflakes. *How silly,* she thought. *All this fuss over a few measly little snowflakes.*

❄ ❄ ❄ ❄ ❄

A few days later, Amy was at the skating rink going through her program. As much as was possible, she had become used to the pain while she skated. Today, however, it seemed to be almost unbearable. Amy found she was having trouble performing even the simplest jumps. Her feet hurt so badly that she felt she almost couldn't think.

She managed to make it through her program until the double salchow. Amy skated backward, doing crossovers, then stepped into a forward three-turn* to set up the jump. But as she attempted to lift into the air, a sharp pain sent her sprawling onto the ice.

Amy couldn't understand what had happened. For a few minutes she seemed unable to move. Finally, she got up slowly and hobbled off the ice.

When she reached the lobby, Amy began unlacing her skates as fast as she could. Tears were flowing down her cheeks. She didn't even notice that Shannon and Kristen had followed her.

"Amy, your feet!" cried Shannon. Amy looked down. Her feet were blue from wearing boots too small.

Kristen's face was full of concern. "How long have your skates been hurting you?"

"For several weeks," Amy admitted. "I thought I could keep skating in them, but . . ." She stopped, unable to go on.

"You can't go on skating in these," warned Kristen. "You'll damage your feet."

"You have to have new skates!" insisted Shannon.

"But I can't," cried Amy, relieved to be pouring out the whole story. "My dad lost his job last week. The only money I have for skating is my baby-sitting money, and I'm just barely paying for my ice time." Amy burst into tears. She was ashamed of crying in front of her friends, but she just couldn't help it.

Shannon and Kristen didn't say anything at first. Finally, Kristen spoke. "Amy, you have to have new skates. We're going to pray that God will provide you with skates that fit."

Amy turned angrily toward her friend. "Pray!" she exclaimed, louder than she had intended. "Do you think God is going to hand me skates, just like that? I don't even have money to buy a decent *used* pair."

"If God wants you to skate," said Kristen, "He can give you skates."

Amy shook her head. "Pray if you want to. But if God wanted me to skate, He wouldn't have let my father get crippled and lose his job. God doesn't care about my family! You've always had it so easy. You can skate as much as you like, with new skates and lessons and freestyles. You don't know what it's like to lose everything you've worked for!"

Kristen and Shannon sat there, stunned. They didn't know what to say. Amy stuck her bruised feet in her shoes and threw her skates in her bag. She knew she had said things she shouldn't have, but she didn't care. She grabbed her bag and hobbled to the door.

Before she left, Kristen touched her arm. "I'm sorry, Amy. But God really does care. And we do, too."

"Thanks," said Amy coldly. She limped out of the rink, away from her friends. It made her angry that she couldn't stop crying. She knew she couldn't skate again in her old skates. She wondered if she would ever come back.

Twelve

It was still thirty minutes before time to go home, but Amy was in no hurry. With her red nose and swollen eyes, she knew she would have to face her family's questions. The long wait also gave her time to think. Amy had treated her friends badly, and she felt guilty. Shannon and Kristen had only been trying to help. Yet there was really nothing they could do.

The competition was only three weeks away. Amy thought it over very carefully. She could see no way to get new skates. Even if she saved all her baby-sitting money, it would still take many months to have enough.

Would it be possible for her family to help out? Amy dismissed that idea immediately. Dad still did not have a job. Money would be very tight until he found something, and that probably would not happen very soon.

Should she give up skating? It was a choice Amy had never considered before. For so long skating had been such an important part of her life. Giving it up seemed almost unthinkable. But Amy knew that her family could not afford the kind of training she had had before her father's accident. And baby-sitting would never earn enough.

Of course, without skating practice there would be more time for school activities and just being with her friends. Amy had really enjoyed being involved with the art club. That wouldn't have been possible if she had been skating every day.

Besides, her family needed her help at home. With Mom working and Dad trying to find a job, they didn't have much time to keep up with the cooking and laundry. Although Grandmother Pederson sometimes helped out, she couldn't be there all the time.

But in spite of everything, Amy knew that she wasn't really ready to give up skating—not yet, anyway.

❄ ❄ ❄ ❄ ❄

It was dark when Grandmother Pederson arrived, so she didn't notice Amy's tear-streaked face. "How was practice?" she asked as Amy climbed into the car.

"Fine, Gram," replied Amy, attempting to sound cheerful. To change the subject, she began talking about school. She was glad it was a short ride home.

Mom and Dad were in the kitchen, and Kurt was watching television in the den when Amy arrived home. She slipped upstairs to her room before anyone saw her, deposited her things on her bed, and hurried into the bathroom. Splashing some water on her face and running a comb through her hair, she attempted to erase the evidence of her terrible afternoon.

Somehow Amy made it through dinner without anyone noticing her swollen eyes. To her relief, no one even asked her about skating. After she finished helping with the dishes, she went to her room to work on homework and started on her math assignment. Math was not her favorite subject, but it did take a lot of concentration. *Maybe this will keep my mind off skating,* she thought. But before she had completed the third problem on the page, she heard the phone ring.

"Amy, telephone," called her mother.

Oh, no, thought Amy. *I hope it's not Shannon or Kristen.* "Hello?"

"Hello, Amy, this is Kristen."

"Oh, hi." She made an effort to make her voice sound normal.

"Are you okay?" Kristen sounded really anxious.

"Um, yeah, I'm okay, I guess." Amy paused. She knew what she needed to do, but it was hard. "I'm sorry about what I said this afternoon," she finally blurted out.

"That's okay. I know you were just upset."

"Well, I'm sorry I acted that way."

"It's all right," said Kristen. "Listen, I thought of something after I got home. I've got a couple of old pairs of skates. They're pretty worn out, but why don't you try them on to see if they fit?"

Suddenly, Amy felt hopeful again. "Really? That would be great!"

"When can you try them on? I would bring them over tonight, but I've got a ton of homework due tomorrow."

"So do I. You'd think the teachers would give us a break this close to Christmas."

"How about tomorrow after school?" asked Kristen. "Can you meet me at the skating rink? That way you can try them out on the ice."

"I'll be there!" said Amy. "And thanks."

Amy felt like jumping up and down as she hung up the phone. She was so excited it was hard to concentrate on finishing math. Maybe skating wasn't over for her after all.

But she wondered why Kristen was being so nice—and after Amy had said such awful things to her. What was it about her friend that made her so different?

❄ ❄ ❄ ❄ ❄

The next afternoon Amy was at the rink before Kristen. It was a little strange waiting there with no skates. But before long Kristen and Shannon both arrived.

"Hi, Amy," said Shannon.

Amy suddenly felt shy. "Hi, Shannon," she said. "I guess I should apologize. I acted pretty terrible yesterday."

"That's okay. I hope Kristen's skates fit," said Shannon.

"Try them on," said Kristen, holding out a pair of skates. As she had said, they looked pretty worn out. Amy sat down and began to put them on, but it was soon obvious that they didn't fit. "They're too big," Amy said, trying to hide the disappointment on her face.

"I have one more pair," said Kristen. "Try these." She held out a pair of skates that looked even more beat up than the others. But Amy didn't care how they looked. She hurriedly unlaced the first pair and began trying on the second.

This time the skates were too tight. She hoped that it was because she wasn't used to them. But as she laced them up she realized that they were just as small as her own skates. "These won't work, either," she announced, disheartened. "They're too tight."

"Why don't you try on the first pair again?" suggested Shannon. "Maybe you could wear thick socks?"

"If she needs thick socks to wear them, they won't do," explained Kristen. "But try them again anyway."

Amy didn't have much hope, but she tried on the first pair again. This time she laced them as tightly as she possibly could, but it didn't do any good. The skates were simply too big. Amy could feel her feet moving around inside them.

"I'm sorry," said Kristen. "These are the only skates I have."

All three girls were quiet. There seemed to be nothing to say. Finally, Amy said, "Thanks for trying. You two go on and skate. I guess I need to get home."

❈ ❈ ❈ ❈ ❈

"I won't be competing in January, after all," Amy announced to her family at supper that night.

"Why not?" asked her mother. She gave Amy a look of concern. "Aren't the lessons with Coach Grischenko working out?"

"Oh, yeah, Coach Grischenko's great." Amy struggled to keep her voice calm. "It's just that my skates are too small. I can't wear them anymore."

"Oh, Amy, I'm sorry," said Mrs. Pederson. "Maybe we can check around and find some used ones until we can help you get new skates."

"I've already tried that. Nearly everyone here is a beginner—nobody has used skates." Amy sighed. "I've really tried to skate again. Maybe I should just give up."

Amy's father looked at her sorrowfully. "I'm sorry, Princess. But things will get better, I promise."

"There'll be more competitions," said Joe. "You've already got enough medals to last a lifetime!"

"Yeah," added Kurt. "I don't see what the big deal is about missing a measly old competition, anyhow."

"Now, Kurt, that's not fair," scolded her mother. "You know it means a lot to Amy."

Amy knew her family was sympathetic, but they didn't understand. Her skating was just not a top priority right now. *Don't they care about my happiness anymore?*

❄ ❄ ❄ ❄ ❄

It was only a few days until Christmas. School was out, and everybody was busy with holiday parties and shopping. Everybody except Amy. She felt as though her world had ended. Without school or skating, she suddenly found herself with too much time on her hands. Much of the time she spent in her room, adding to her collection of skating pictures.

One afternoon Kristen knocked on the Pedersons' front door. "Merry Christmas!" she said cheerfully, as Amy invited her in. Kristen held out a small package, wrapped in a bright Christmas print.

"But I don't have anything for you," protested Amy.

"That's okay. I just wanted you to have this," said Kristen. "Go ahead, open it."

Amy tore open the paper to find a cross-stitched message in a small oval frame. It read: "Enjoy serving the Lord. And he will give you what you want. (Psalm 37:4)."

"It's beautiful," she exclaimed. "Did you make it?"

Kristen nodded. "I learned how to cross-stitch last summer. This Bible verse is special to me, and I wanted you to have it."

"Thank you, Kristen." Amy read the verse over again thoughtfully. "But why this verse?"

"I know how much you want to skate. I wish I could do something to help. I can't, but God can."

Amy sighed. "I'm not so sure. Why should He even care? Nobody else thinks my skating is very important."

"It's important to God. He loves you and cares about you."

Amy read the verse again. "Does this mean that if I believe in God, He'll help me to skate?"

"I don't know. I think it means that if you trust God, He will make things right. I can't promise that God will help you to skate, but if He doesn't, it will be because that's what's best for you."

"Or maybe just the best thing for everybody else."

"No," said Kristen firmly. "He'll do what's best for you."

Amy thought about this for a few moments. She remembered what she had learned in the youth meeting about how God loved us so much that He sent Jesus to die for us . . . about running the race of life to win. It was confusing, but she wondered if she should try.

"What am I supposed to do?" she asked.

"Give your life to Jesus," said Kristen. "That means being sorry for your sins and asking Him to forgive you. Tell Him that you want to belong to Him and be one of His children. He'll help you, He really will."

There was a long moment of silence. "Let me think about it," Amy said finally. Although she thought she wanted what Kristen was talking about, she wasn't sure. She needed some time.

"Sure," said Kristen. "Well, I've got to get home. We're going to visit some relatives tonight."

"Thanks for the picture," said Amy. "I'll hang it in my room." They walked to the door together. "Merry Christmas!"

Amy smiled as they waved good-bye. Although she admired Kristen's faith, she didn't really expect God to help her get skates. After all, He had already taken skating out of her life. Hadn't He?

Thirteen

Kurt picked up a large gingerbread cookie cutter and stuck it in the middle of the rolled-out sugar cookie dough. Carefully, he picked up the cookie and put it on the pan, then pinched off a large piece of extra dough and crammed it in his mouth.

"Kurt!" scolded Amy. "We won't have any cookies to decorate if you eat all the dough."

"I like the dough better."

"You know you're not supposed to eat raw cookie dough," Amy reminded him. She spooned more dough onto the board and started rolling it out.

"This is the last batch," said Amy as she put the pan in the oven. "You can finish decorating them."

"Don't you want to help?" Kurt smeared white icing on a bell-shaped cookie, then sprinkled it with green sugar.

"The job is all yours!" said Amy. "Just don't eat the decorations before they go on the cookies." Usually, she and Kurt took turns decorating cutout cookies in the shapes of bells, stars, angels, and Christmas trees. But somehow baking was not as much fun this year.

By the time the last batch of cookies was out of the oven, Grandmother Pederson had arrived to help with the other Christmas cooking. Amy wandered into the living room. She thought maybe a good old-fashioned Christmas movie would cheer her up. But hearing "White Christmas" just made her more depressed. She looked out the window. In spite of the snowfall a couple of weeks ago, the sun was now shining, and the day looked perfect for a picnic. *Doesn't look much like Christmas,* thought Amy. Suddenly, she was homesick: for skating, for Virginia, for all her old friends, for things the way they used to be.

Amy felt all alone. Everyone else seemed to be having a good time. They hardly seemed to notice that Amy wasn't joining in. Once Grandmother Pederson asked, "Amy, are you feeling all right? You look a little pale."

"I'm fine, Gram," Amy replied. She gave a weak smile and hurried away before her grandmother could ask any more questions. *She wouldn't understand anyway.*

All of a sudden she couldn't stand being in the house another minute. Calling to her father that she was going for a walk, she ran out the door. She had to get away from all this holiday spirit. After all, it was warm enough for springtime outside.

❄ ❄ ❄ ❄ ❄

Amy walked for a long time, not really caring where she was going. She left her own neighborhood and explored areas that were unfamiliar. The fresh air made her feel better, even if it did seem too warm for Christmas.

While she walked, Amy thought things over. She remembered her very first time on ice skates and how much fun it was. She remembered skating in her first competition and the thrill of winning a medal.

Amy was hurt that her family didn't seem to care about her skating. They were so busy worrying about their own problems that they didn't realize how important skating was to her. She wished she could make them see.

Then she remembered the Bible verse that Kristen had given her. "Enjoy serving the Lord. And he will give you what you want."

Does God really care about me? Amy wondered. *Does He care about my skating?* At least Kristen seemed to care. Amy wasn't sure why. Was it her love for God that made her so different?

For a long time she thought about what Kristen had said. *If you love God most of all, He will do what's best for you.* Amy wondered if God would want her to give up skating. But maybe it didn't matter anymore. After all, it looked as though she would never be able to skate again anyway.

Amy stopped and thought again about Kristen's words, "He'll do what's best for you." She had been so busy feeling sorry for herself that she had not noticed all the good things God had given her. Her father was alive and, against the odds, his health was improving. Her family loved her. She had a home and friends. God had been taking care of her all along.

Amy wasn't sure how to ask Jesus to be her Savior, but she would try. *Dear Jesus,* she prayed, *do You really care? Please help me to believe.* She hestitated a moment, then added, *And please be my Savior. Amen.*

❄ ❄ ❄ ❄ ❄

The sun was shining when Amy awoke on Christmas Eve morning, and it promised to be a beautiful warm day. She looked out her window and frowned. It didn't look like there was the faintest chance of a white Christmas, but somehow she didn't care. Even though she was sad that she couldn't skate, she felt tingly—happy about her new faith in God.

❄ ❄ ❄ ❄ ❄

Later in the afternoon the doorbell rang. "I'll get it!" shouted Amy as she went to the door. To her surprise, it was Shannon and Kristen.

"Merry Christmas!" Shannon announced cheerfully. "We thought you needed some of our specially baked cookies to cheer you up." She held up a plate of decorated Christmas cookies. "Besides, it was a good excuse to come see you. We've missed you."

Amy invited her friends inside. "Thanks, guys. I've missed you, too. The cookies look great. Did you really make them yourselves?"

"Kristen did most of the baking," admitted Shannon. "But I decorated them."

"I'm surprised there are any decorations left," put in Kristen. "Shannon ate more candies than she put on the cookies!"

Amy laughed. "You sound just like Kurt! They look good, anyway. I think I'd better try one." She picked up a cookie, but before she could take a bite, the doorbell rang again. "Now, who could that be?" She put down her cookie and went to the door.

"Package for Amy Pederson." A deliveryman held a large package wrapped in brown paper. Amy signed for it and brought it into the room. Her face lit up with expectation. "It must be for Christmas." She looked at the address curiously. "Now, what could Elizabeth have sent me? This box is really heavy."

"Open it now," insisted Shannon, bouncing up and down with excitement. "We want to see what it is."

Amy sat down and began to rip open the package. It was a box that had contained skates at one time. *Could it be?* Amy held her breath. *Had God answered her prayer?*

Amy opened the box. "Skates!" she shouted, and Shannon and Kristen squealed with delight. It was a pair of skates, not new, but almost new. Amy couldn't believe it. She held them up, her eyes filling with tears she was trying not to let fall.

There was a letter in the box, and Amy picked it up and quickly read it.

Dear Amy,

I only wore these skates two months before I out-grew them. I hope they'll fit you. Merry Christmas

Love,
Elizabeth

"It's from my friend Elizabeth in Virginia," said Amy, after reading the note. "She says she outgrew these."

"Try them on!" exclaimed Shannon. "Let's see if they fit."

Amy's heart stopped. In her excitement she had almost forgotten that the skates wouldn't be any good to her if they didn't fit. Of course, they wouldn't fit. It was too good to be true.

However, she dutifully pulled off her shoes and began lacing up the first boot. Amy told herself not to get excited; she was so afraid of being disappointed.

When she got the first skate on, Amy wiggled the boot. Then she stood and put her weight on it. Finally, she smiled. "I think it fits."

"Hooray!" shouted Shannon and Kristen.

By that time Amy noticed that her mother and father had come in and were smiling at each other. "Did you know about this?" Amy demanded.

"No, we didn't know anything about it," said her dad. "But somehow we just knew something would work out."

Kristen didn't say anything, but her eyes were shining. Amy still couldn't believe that she had skates, skates that fit. She put on the other boot just to be sure. There was no question about it; the skates fit as well as if they had been made for her.

"Is the rink open this afternoon?" Amy asked.

"Yes, it is," said Kristen. "Let's go skate."

Amy looked at her parents pleadingly. "Do you mind? I really want to try out my new skates."

"Go ahead," said Mr. Pederson. "You haven't exactly been full of Christmas spirit this year anyway, you know." He winked.

So they *had* noticed her unhappiness. Amy was a little ashamed of herself for thinking they didn't care. And she began to realize that she hadn't exactly been pleasant.

But right now she was gloriously happy. Alone in her room to get ready for skating, she stopped for a minute. *Thank You for my skates, God,* she prayed. *You really do care!*

❊ ❈ ❊ ❈ ❊

In half an hour Amy met Shannon and Kristen at the rink. The rink wasn't very crowded that afternoon. But the girls didn't get much practicing done anyway; they had a wonderful time just playing around on the ice. The blades on Amy's "new" skates needed to be sharpened, but otherwise they were perfect.

"I have something to tell you guys," Amy said shyly when the girls were getting ready to go home. Shannon looked up curiously, but Kristen just smiled. "Last night, I asked Jesus to be my Savior."

Kristen reached over and hugged Amy.

❄ ❄ ❄ ❄ ❄

The rest of that Christmas was very special for Amy. Of course Gram and Grandpa Pederson were staying for Christmas Eve supper. Amy enjoyed telling them all about her "new" skates.

Amy pitched in to help with the cooking and even the cleaning up. She decided that she needed to make up for putting a damper on everyone's Christmas spirit! When the family sang carols after supper, Amy joined in. She had never paid much attention to the words of her favorite carols before, but now she understood what they were talking about.

Later that evening, after everyone had gone home or off to bed, Amy sat alone on her bed watching the stars out the window. She remembered making Christmas wishes on the first star when she was small. But this year her Christmas wish had come true. And as she dropped off to sleep on that Christmas Eve night, she thought about a very special star of long ago that shone brightly over a little child in Bethlehem.

Fourteen

January 3

Dear Elizabeth,

Thank you so much for the skates. They fit per-fectly. Did you know that your skates were an answer to prayer? I asked God for skates, and right after that your skates came in the mail. Now that I have skates, I'll be able to compete. I can't wait. The competition is this weekend.

Love,
Amy

The day of the competition drew near, and Amy began practicing her program in earnest. She only had three days a week to practice, but she made the most of her time on the ice. Often she came home drenched with perspiration in spite of the cold air in the ice rink.

Yet she still found time to help Shannon with her program. Amy was really proud of her pupil. Shannon was becoming a beautiful skater. Even though her program consisted of relatively simple jumps and spins, she had a special quality that made her lovely to watch.

As hard as Amy tried, she couldn't help being a bit jealous of Kristen. Amy sighed as she watched her practice her program. Kristen was a perfectionist in all that she did, and it showed in her skating.

Still, Amy was glad to be competing again. She wished she could have more practice time and lessons, but she was so happy to be skating at all that she didn't really care if Kristen beat her. At least not very much.

❋ ❋ ❋ ❋ ❋

The rink was a hub of activity when Amy arrived for the competition on Saturday morning. A number of people were sitting on bleachers set up at the side of the rink, and others were rushing here and there. There were skaters wandering around in their costumes, coaches giving last-minute instructions, and mothers fixing little girls' hair. Amy wasn't scheduled to skate until four o'clock, but Shannon and Tiffany were both skating in the morning.

"Amy! Over here!" Amy saw Kristen waving to her from a seat on the bleachers.

"Hi, Kristen. Have you seen Shannon and Tiffany?"

Kristen shook her head. "I'm sure they're here somewhere. I think Tiffany's group is up next."

"Please welcome Bethany Pitts . . ." boomed an announcer as Amy sat down. The music started and a tiny girl in the center of the ice began her program. She looked as though she couldn't be more than four years old. The small child skated slowly forward, using her arms and hands to express the music. Then she skated backward and finally came to a stop and curtsied to the crowd. "Isn't she adorable?" Kristen remarked.

"Amy! Kristen! Boy, am I glad to see you two." Shannon's face was white, and she was actually shaking. "I'm so nervous. I don't think I can do this."

Amy and Kristen exchanged looks. They had been competing so long that they had forgotten how scary a first competition could be.

Kristen took charge. "Shannon, everybody is nervous their first time. You'll be fine as soon as you start your program."

Shannon looked unconvinced. "I've never been in front of a crowd before. What if I mess up? I'll just die!"

"You won't mess up," said Kristen firmly. "But if you do make a mistake, just jump up and start skating again."

"Do I look all right?"

"You look beautiful!" said Amy. Shannon's short dark hair and Asian features gave a look of elegance to the lacy pink costume Amy had loaned her.

"Sit down and watch the little kids with us," said Kristen. "If those little kids can do it, so can you. Where's Tiffany?"

"She's waiting with her coach," said Shannon. She pointed to a waiting area on the other side of the rink. "It's almost time for her to skate."

There was still a little time before Tiffany's program. While they waited, Kristen pointed out some of the coaches and skaters she had seen at other competitions. As an experienced competitor, she had many stories to tell. Before long, Shannon relaxed and grew interested in listening.

"Let's welcome Tiffany Roberts." The girls turned to watch Tiffany skate into position at the center of the ice. Her Bavarian-style costume went perfectly with "The Lonely Goatherd" from *The Sound of Music*. It was a simple program consisting mostly of forward glides and backward swizzles, but Tiffany performed it like a pro. Her long dark ponytail bobbed up and down as she used her arms to express the music. Tiffany loved an audience, and it showed. She handled herself like an experienced entertainer, curtsying to all sides of the ice before exiting with a flourish.

The girls joined Shannon's parents to wait for Tiffany. They were all thrilled with how well she had done, and Tiffany was obviously pleased with herself. She came prancing up to them with Susan Barnes, her coach. "Did you get me flowers?" she demanded, and they all laughed and gave her the flowers they had brought for her.

When the results were posted, Tiffany had placed second. "Do you want to see my medal?" she asked everyone she met the rest of the day.

Soon it was Shannon's turn. "We'll be praying for you to do your best," whispered Kristen before they sent her off with Coach Barnes to wait in the holding area.

"Now *I'm* nervous!" said Amy. "I hope Shannon skates well." The girls couldn't bear to sit down, so they jumped up and stood at the side of the rink to watch. There were five skaters competing in Shannon's group. The girls watched anxiously as the first two skaters completed their programs. Shannon would skate third.

"Please welcome Shannon Roberts." Shannon skated to her starting position, looking white and scared. Over the speakers came the first notes of the *Star Wars* theme, but Shannon hesitated for a long moment. Amy caught her breath, wondering if her friend was going to skate. Surely she hadn't forgotten her program!

Finally, Shannon skated cautiously forward, a serious expression on her face. Her first move was a waltz jump*. Taking off from a left forward edge, she made a half turn in the air and landed shakily on a right backward edge.

"Go, Shannon!" Amy and Kristen shouted encouragement. A slight smile crossed Shannon's face, and she seemed to relax. Carefully and smoothly, she continued her routine, exhibiting the attention to detail she had gained from her friends' instruction. After she ended with a great two-foot spin, Shannon finally smiled.

Amy and Kristen jumped up and down, making as much noise as they could. "Shannon, you were super!" they shouted as she joined them.

Shannon wore a look of relief. "I'm so glad it's over." She sat down and began to take off her skates. In a moment her parents came over, and they all waited anxiously for the results.

It wasn't a long wait, but it seemed to take forever. Shannon couldn't bear to look, so Kristen and Amy took turns checking to see if the result sheets had been posted. Finally, Kristen came running back from the lobby, squealing. "Shannon, you've won second place!"

"Me? Are you sure?" Shannon's face registered disbelief.

"It's true. Come see for yourself."

The girls raced to the wall in the lobby where the result sheets were posted. There it was: Second place, Shannon Roberts.

"Now aren't you glad we talked you into this?" teased Amy.

"I guess it wasn't so bad," admitted Shannon with a smile. "But I'm still glad it's over!"

❋ ❋ ❋ ❋ ❋

The girls went out for a quick lunch with the Roberts family, but they had to hurry back to the rink for Kevin's program. They were just in time to wish him luck.

"Thanks," said Kevin, giving them a brief glance while adjusting his skates. "I think I'm ready for this."

"Whoa!" said Kristen. "You're pretty confident."

Kevin grinned at Amy and Shannon. Then he turned to his sister. "I promised to show you some real skating."

"You're going to need some luck!" retorted Kristen.

Amy and Shannon exchanged looks. They all knew that Kevin goofed off at practices, although he spent as much time on the ice as Kristen did. Kevin was skating next, so they hurried to find a seat.

It was a different Kevin who took the ice from the one girls usually saw. He skated confidently into position, with perfect posture and head held high. As the music started, he launched into his program, completing every jump. A flying camel* ended the program, and Kevin finished it off with a salute to the judges.

"Wow!" Shannon's dark eyes were wide. "I never knew Kevin was so good."

Amy, puzzled by Kevin's amazing performance, said, "I've never seen Kevin skate like that!"

Kristen shook her head in annoyance. "He always does this," she fumed. "Blows off practices and then skates great in competition. I can't stand it!"

Oh, thought Amy with secret satisfaction, *so I'm not the only one who gets jealous.*

❄ ❄ ❄ ❄ ❄

Finally, it was Amy's and Kristen's turns to skate. Amy changed into her costume, a blue dress with rhinestones. Suddenly, she felt really nervous. Although she had been in many competitions in the past, she had always had the benefit of many hours of lessons and special choreography*. She was happy to be competing, but she knew she wasn't really ready. Those weeks without skates had cost a lot of practice time.

Amy was trying not to be envious of Kristen, but it was hard. She glanced at her friend. Dressed in a sparkly green chiffon dress that complemented her curly auburn hair, Kristen looked stunning. And Amy knew that her program was just as stunning.

Just then Kristen turned around. "Why don't we pray together?" she asked. Amy was surprised, but she nodded, and the girls bowed their heads together.

"Dear Father," Kristen prayed, "help us to skate our best today. But most of all, help us to honor You."

Then Kristen gave Amy a quick hug. "Good luck!"

Amy suddenly realized that Kristen wasn't thinking about beating her or anyone else. Her goal was to honor God. Wasn't that what the hockey star had talked about? Running the race to win—not to win a medal, but to honor God. "Thanks, Kristen. Same to you." She smiled, and she found that she wasn't nearly as nervous now. "Let's go skate!" she said.

❅ ❅ ❅ ❅ ❅

As Amy headed for her starting position, she felt again the thrill of performing on the ice. It was great to be skating again, whether she won or not. Her music started, and Amy forgot about judges, medals, and being jealous of Kristen. For the moment, nothing mattered but giving enjoyment to the people watching her skate.

And she was having a great time. Always before, Amy had been so focused on winning that she couldn't really enjoy performing. This time she was having fun, and it showed. Her program had a lot of footwork, and Amy completed the complicated turns with precision.

Everything was going great until she missed her double salchow jump*. She was tilted in the air and came down sideways and crashed into the ice. For just a moment, her heart almost stopped. She couldn't believe she had missed the jump. Amy scrambled up as quickly as she could and tried to put the missed jump behind her. She needed to concentrate on her last big move, the double toe-single loop combination jump. This time she nailed both jumps. As the music swung into the final notes, Amy ended with a fast one-foot spin*. She curtsied to the audience and the judges, feeling fairly pleased with her performance. She could have skated better with more practice, of course, but she had done her best with what she had to work with.

Her family was waiting with hugs and flowers after she finished, but there was no time for congratulations. It was Kristen's turn to skate. Amy and Shannon watched from the side of the rink as she began her program.

Even though Amy had seen Kristen's program many times before, she watched in amazement as her friend performed alone on the ice to the Tchaikovsky ballet music that suited her so well. Beautiful spirals*, spread eagles*, and layback spins* were Kristen's specialty. But she managed to land every jump as well. Amy forgot to be jealous. By the time Kristen had finished, Amy was certain that she had won first place. And she was happy for her. She knew that Kristen deserved it.

"You both were wonderful!" said Shannon when Kristen joined them. "I hope I can skate like that sometime."

"You skated great, Kristen," agreed Amy. "You deserve to get first."

"Thanks, but don't be too sure. There were some other good skaters, including you!"

Together the three girls waited for the results. It seemed an eternity before they were posted. When they were finally up, Shannon ran to look.

"Kristen won first, and Amy's third!" she shouted as she ran back to her friends. "Congratulations! You'll both get a medal."

Kristen looked at Amy and grinned. "It's a sweep. Among the three of us, we've got gold, silver, and bronze."

Amy smiled back. It was hard to explain, but she felt as though she had won more than a medal.

Fifteen

"Go, Amy!" shouted Kristen. It was almost a month after the competition, and Amy was finally landing her double lutz. At least, she was landing it occasionally. She gave Kristen a thumbs-up and circled the ice, preparing for another attempt. Skating backward straight into the corner of the rink, Amy reached back and jabbed her right toe pick into the ice. Vaulting into the air, she rotated two full turns and landed on her right blade.

"Way to go, Amy!" Kristen cheered. "A perfect landing!"

Amy grinned. "I can't believe I'm finally landing that jump—again!" She skated to a stop next to her friend. "I had just started landing the double lutz when I had to quit skating."

"Next thing I know you'll be landing the double axel," teased Kristen. "And I'll still be mopping up the ice."

"But you nearly have it!" protested Amy. "You almost landed it yesterday—I saw you."

Kristen sighed. "Coach Grischenko said I could land it if I believed I could. But I think it takes more than belief."

Amy laughed. "I know. She gives me that line, too. But you really are close."

"Shannon is going to catch up with both of us before we know it," said Kristen. The girls watched as Shannon did a toe loop jump*. It was only a single jump, but she made it look beautiful. Shannon continued to amaze her coach and everyone else with her progress.

Amy nodded in agreement. "She is going to be a really good skater."

"What about me?" asked Tiffany. The girls looked down to see Shannon's little sister listening. "Am I a good skater, too?"

Kristen laughed. "Yes, you're a good skater, too."

"Do you want to see what I can do?"

"Okay, Tiff, we're watching," said Amy.

Tiffany took a few strokes and squatted down on her skates, then stuck one leg out in front. She held this position for a few seconds, then tumbled to the ice.

"That was a great shoot-the-duck*, Tiff!" said Kristen. "We're impressed."

Tiffany had become something of a rink mascot. She was so cute she was hard to resist. Although Tiff was making slow and steady progress, she found it hard to concentrate on practicing. There were just too many people to talk to!

"Kevin! Do you want to see me do my shoot-the-duck?" Kevin was stepping off the ice when Tiffany cornered him.

"Okay, Tiff. I'll do it with you." Kevin stepped back on the ice and performed a shoot-the-duck. Tiffany giggled and followed him.

The two of them glided down the ice in a squat position and landed in two heaps at the end of the ice. Amy and Kristen laughed as they watched.

"Kevin finally found somebody his own age to play with," said Kristen.

Amy just smiled. She thought it was nice of Kevin to play with Tiffany, even if he was a pest at times.

Kristen reached down to tighten her skate laces. "Well, it's back to the double axel," she said.

"You're going to land it soon, I just know it," promised Amy. She gave Kristen a high-five and headed back to the center of the rink.

Amy skated to another area of the ice to work on her own jumps. Practice time was valuable these days. Baby-sitting jobs had been scarce since Christmas, and she had only been able to pay for two practices a week. In the meantime, she stayed busy with the art club and the Saturday night youth meetings. It was frustrating to try to keep skating. Sometimes she wondered if it was worth it. But every time she got back on the ice, she knew she just couldn't quit.

***** *

One afternoon Amy came home from school instead of going to the rink as she had planned. When she walked in the front door, her father was standing in the living room, out of his wheelchair. Amy stopped and stared in surprise as her father grinned back at her. For a moment she couldn't say anything.

"What are you doing?" she finally asked.

"I was hoping to surprise everyone," explained Mr. Pederson, "but I guess the secret's out. I'm walking!" He leaned against the wall. "I get tired very quickly, though."

Amy dropped her things and ran over to help him. "Are you okay? Shall I get your chair?" She felt panicky. Her father had been in a wheelchair for so long; she wasn't sure if it was safe for him to be getting around.

"I'm fine," he assured her. "I've been walking for a few weeks now."

"Does Mom know?" Amy was still concerned.

"No, I wanted it to be a surprise." He stood up straight again. "I guess you'd better get my chair. I've walked more than I should this afternoon."

Amy got the wheelchair and helped her father get into it. At first, she could only feel relief to have him safely seated again. However, once he was back in his chair, she realized what this meant. *Dad is walking again! Could it really be true?*

Mr. Pederson took a few deep breaths; then he looked at her. "Amy, I know the last couple of years have been really hard for you," he began. "But lately you've been doing so much better. I can see that skating again has really been good for you."

Amy looked down. She had not yet told her parents about becoming a Christian. But she knew she needed to say something now. "Dad, I've been learning about God and how living for Him is more important than anything." She paused, unsure of what to say next.

Her father looked thoughtful. "I kind of thought it was something like that." He sighed heavily. "I guess I've gotten pretty far away from God." He shook his head. There was pain in his eyes. "I even blamed Him for my accident."

Amy waited for her father to finish. *He felt just like I did,* she thought.

Her father continued. "I guess it's time I started putting God first in my life. Thanks for reminding me, Amy." He reached out to give her a hug.

Amy felt happier than she had in a long time. Not only had she found a special faith in Jesus, but now she could share it with her family.

Mr. Pederson grinned. "Want to know a secret?" Amy nodded, smiling. "This is something else your mother doesn't know about yet. I haven't told anyone because I wanted to be sure it was firm. But since things have been hardest on you, I think maybe I will go ahead and tell you. One of my old clients is opening a new branch in the Dallas area. They've offered me a job."

Amy looked worried. "But you can't travel."

"I won't have to. This is something I can do in the office. And they have offered me more money than what I was making before the accident."

"Oh, Dad, that's wonderful!" Amy hugged her father. It seemed too good to be true. Things were really getting better, at last.

"So I guess this means you can begin serious skating training again soon." Mr. Pederson looked at her quizzically. "That is, if it's really what you want."

For just a moment, Amy hesitated. Was it really what she wanted? So much had changed during the last few months. She thought about all she had learned: about winning, about friendship, and about the things that are really important. Amy had discovered that there are more important things in life even than skating: like knowing Jesus.

But she didn't hesitate long. Even though she had been willing to give it up, God was giving her the chance to skate again. It seemed too good to be true.

Amy gave her father a big hug. "Yes, Dad, it's what I really want."